Her Boss

Valerie Colson

Contents

Chapter One

Senior year.

So many events happen in a mere year—not even a whole year. So many teens await this day that they are finally seniors in high school.

Be it the popularity—and therefore seniority—that other teens dream for, or possibly the promise of a huge prom they finally get to attend; perhaps the fact that it brings them one step closer to leaving school. Whatever the reason may be, senior year is also hectic; what with the students hysterically trying to find out what they want to do with their lives whilst also trying to get good grades in order to graduate.

That year of high school is supposed to be the best, if not full of stress. The seniors get to attend the prom, they pull the senior pranks, of course they all party for some unkown reason, and then they finally graduate. Leaving behind all those friends, and being released into the world as adults after attending school for nearly their entire lives from age six to eighteen.

Though my experience was completely different, abnormal. My experience of senior year changed drastically one fateful Wednesday morning during my fifth period class. That small, seemingly insignificant hour of class would prove to change my entire life.

~ ~ ~

I doodle in boredom on my notebook, wishing my best friend Lydia was in this class so I can pass notes behind the teacher's back. I sigh lightly, zoning back in to listen to my droning teacher—Ms. Stine.

"This month is Parent Appreciation month, now everyone knows what that means. Each one of you will shadow one of your parents for the month, it doesn't matter which parent you shadow but I urge you all to choose the parent whose job would interest you the most." Ms. Stine announces when I zone back into her boring lecture. Of course, the entire class erupts in a chorus of loud groans at the announcement.

We've all heard the rumors from the other seniors about Parent Appreciation month, and we all saw the date in our syllabus we got on the first day of school last semester. It wouldn't be such a horrible ordeal if all we had to do was stay at work with our parents, but that's not all we're suppose to do, according to the other seniors. We all blew it off though, as immature teenagers do, which was probably a stupid move on our behalf.

"I do not want to hear any of that groaning, you all knew this was coming. I suggest you all take a lot of notes because after the month is over you will hand in a fifteen page paper about what your parent does, what their job title is, and how efficient the workplace is in general. I'll give you all a hand-out now about what should and should not be in the paper, so there will be no excuse if you fail to turn in a proper paper." She adds and continues after passing out a large packet of papers for the project.

"Along with the paper you will give a ten minute oral presentation about what they do and how the month went. You'll turn in the report on the first of next month, the same day you will give your speech. Of course,

I shouldn't have to tell you this but I don't want you to write in fifty point font and hope it passes because that will be an automatic fail. You must write in MLA format, twelve point font in Times New Roman." She pauses to give us time to complain but we all know better than to argue or complain.

"When you turn in your paper it will be like all the others we have completed this year. You will turn in your notes, an outline, a rough draft that shows the correction marks, and the final polished paper. You will all have different schedules due to the fact that all your parents will work different hours so I have already worked out a schedule. All of you will come to school in the morning, wait until lunch than leave during lunch to shadow your parents. This will give you enough time every day to observe their working habits. Those of you whose parents work at night will have to come see me after class to get a schedule. You'll receive all the homework for your other classes every morning so as not to miss anything." We all nod even though it's obvious more than half of us don't want to do this. Of course, she continues before we can ask any questions about the wretched assignment.

"It will start tomorrow, on the first to make this a full month. This is worth half your grade, so do well. But it's also a requirement to pass my class. So if you somehow have managed to keep your grade at one hundred percent during last semester along with this semester you will still fail the class if you don't pass this assignment. I will fail you if I feel you didn't pay enough attention and put in enough effort into everything. So pay attention." She adds sternly and we all nod once more. She then goes into detail of what we need in our presentations and papers, explaining the packet she gave us page by page.

When the bell finally rings the entire class leaves in such a hurry I'm surprised there isn't vapor trails in their absence. I lazily walk out the door last, ignoring the other students that are pushing around to get to the cafeteria for lunch. I slowly head to the feeding room myself, only stopping when someone jumps on my back. I sigh and cringe when Lydia all but screams in my ears, causing them to ring.

"Onward march, Lev!" Lydia points in the direction of the cafeteria in determination while I continue to just stand there in the hall.

"What are you doing, Mary?" I tease, leaning back in an attempt to throw her off my back but to no avail. She groans, jumps off my back then continues to walk beside me as we walk to the cafeteria.

"You know I don't like being called Mary, it sounds Holy." She shudders and I laugh. She hates being called Mary, her parents are—to say the least—very religious Catholics so naturally they named her after the Virgin Mary.

Of course, she's anything but Holy, she's an atheist which her parents hate and try to "fix" on a daily basis. She's also not into guys, which her parents also try to "fix" on a daily basis. When she came out they freaked out on her, and now look to her younger brother to make them proud. And as like the stereotypical Catholic girl, she's a tad bit promiscuous. She's also long since basically changed her name to her middle name, Lydia. No one ever calls her by her first name, mainly because she gets so mad when people do.

"I guess it is ironic considering you've slept with almost everyone in school." I muse and she grins.

"Oh please, I haven't slept with everyone. I haven't slept with you." She winks and I roll my eyes. If she wasn't my best friend, I would probably get pissed at her for saying that. Though, we've known each other since first grade, our parents have been best friends since high school so we grew up around each other. We're usually inseparable but this year we were placed in two different classes, but I don't mind too much.

She's incredibly weird though, and quite perverted. Not to mention sarcastic. Her hair color changes on a weekly basis, one time she dyed it bright pink. She also draws attention to herself by wearing god awful neon colors that don't match at all. It really amazes me that she's not messed with at school, at all. Then again, that could be because she's into martial arts and can incapacitate someone in less time than it would take to scream.

"So, what's new?" she questions brightly and I sigh, deciding to tell her about the assignment in English. That's one of the two classes we don't have together so she doesn't know about the horrid assignment yet.

"You know how everybody said one day we would shadow our parents? And we just blew it off?" I question and she nods for me to continue, her fake purple eyes glancing away from some girl to stare back at me.

"Well, that day has come. I just wanted to warn you." I add as we walk through the cafeteria doors. The smell of food assaults my nostrils while the sound of chattering students fill my ears, making me cringe slightly at the assault on my senses.

"Shit." She curses in dismay about my news. We step up to the lunch line to wait but a perky blonde chick, who admittedly is gorgeous, cuts in front of us.

"Excuse me." I snap in irritation and she turns to look at me, sizing me up.

"Yes?" She purrs, her voice a bit too high for my liking.

"Look, just because you're pretty doesn't mean you can cut in line. We were here first, and if you don't move I'll move you myself." Lydia snaps before I can open my mouth to ask her politely to move. She huffs, glares at Lydia but goes back to the back of the line anyway. I arch a brow in question at Lydia, wondering if she's in a bad mood or just irritated with the blonde.

"Don't you think that was a bit harsh?" I question. She rolls her eyes and shakes her head, waving me off, uninterested.

"Nope." She states and smiles brightly when we get to the food line. We grab our food and sit down at our usual table in the middle of the crowded lunch room.

I stare at my food fondly, wondering briefly if I eat too much but those thoughts are washed away as I take the first bite of the junk food that will surely lead to an early death.

"Lev, you look like you're ready to make love to your food." Lydia states, laughing a bit. I glance over at her and grin.

"Just admiring it." I reply. She shakes her head and rolls her eyes but continues to eat her own food. As I take another bite of the heavenly food our other friend—Jessica—sits at the table. Lydia glances at her then grins.

"Jess, doesn't Lev look like he's two seconds from screwing his food?" Lydia asks and Jess shrugs. I send a glare at Lydia but she swiftly ignores it while Jess takes in my appearance.

"We--" Jess starts but I moan, rather loudly, cutting her off because the food is just so amazing.

"I mean, I was going to say no, but I think I've just been proven wrong." Jess muses and I shrug it off, continuing to dig into my food. After we're finished I begin working on math while Jess and Lydia chat about random things that I honestly couldn't care less about. I zone out momentarily, ignoring them, until I hear my name come up so I focus on their conversation again.

"So, Lydia. Did Lev tell you about the new assignment in English?" Jess questions Lydia who groans.

"Yes, it's horrible." She grumbles over-dramatically just as the lunch bell rings, indicating lunch is over. We all go our separate way, and I end up falling asleep in a few of my less important classes. When the last bell rings it's like music to my ears.

When I get out to the parking lot I notice Lydia and Jess waiting in front of my midnight blue Camaro. Unfortunately, I'm their ride to and from school, which can get irritating but at least I don't have to go out of my way to drop them off. We all get in, turning on the radio. I drop Jess home first and glance at Lydia.

"So, home or did you want to hang?" I question, because most of the time she'll hang around my house after school to avoid her parents. She seems to think about it for a few minutes but shakes her head.

"Home, I've got homework to do. Not to mention we both have to get ready for the job shadowing assignment." She adds with a heavy sigh and I nod sorrowfully at that.

"I hate that you're right." I mumble and drop her off at her house. When I get home I go straight to my dad who's sitting at the couch reading the paper.

"Hey Dad. I need to shadow you this month." He stares at me for a moment, processing my abrupt words.

"Why?" He asks curiously.

"A school assignment. I have to leave school at lunch, spend the day at your work and write a report about it." I explain and he nods slowly, thoughtfully. Then he shrugs and turns towards the direction of the stairs.

"Sheryl," Dad calls and my mom comes into the room not five minutes later.

"Hm?" My mom hums in question, her hazel eyes that I inherited glancing at my dad curiously.

"Lev is going to shadow you for the month." He states, glancing down at the paper innocently while both my mom and I stare at him in confusion.

"But I want to shadow you, your job is fun." I add and he looks up at me once more.

"Nah, all I do is sit at a desk and order people to demolish buildings. Plus, my colleagues are old, all in their sixties. While your mother's colleagues, on the other hand, are much closer to your age. They're still in their twenties, some are even your age, you'll get along with them better." He explains and I continue to stare at him.

"She sits in a desk all day, too." I state. He shrugs, turning back to the paper again.

"You're shadowing your mother, don't argue. Now, go do your homework." He orders without glancing at me and I roll my eyes, obeying his order. I finish all my homework by eleven so I get ready for bed, praying my dad is right and I'll get along with my mom's colleagues when I meet them tomorrow.

Chapter Two

{ Chapter Two}

I wake up to a cover of some song and groan, slamming my hand on the alarm clock. My sheets cling to my sweaty body, making me question just what I had been dreaming about. I don't think it was a nightmare, it doesn't feel like it. If anything I feel like it was a good dream. Those thoughts quickly flee my mind though when my phone rings. I pick it up, knowing it's Lydia seeing as she's the only one who would dare to call me this early.

"Hey, Lyd." I greet.

"Damn, how do you always know it's me?" Lydia questions in honest surprise and wonder. I roll my eyes, sliding out of the bed to get clothes ready for a shower.

"I'm psychic, now why did you call?" I demand, tossing a gray shirt onto my bed before I realize I probably should try to look a bit more professional considering I have to go to Mom's work. Then again, I hate dressing up so I won't bother.

"Can you pick me up? My mom left already and my dad's car got impounded so I need a ride." Lydia explains, breaking me from my earlier thoughts and sending surprise rushing through me.

"Impounded? How?" I inquire, grabbing a pair of jeans and a clean pair of black boxers before I head into my bathroom. I put the phone on speaker for a few minutes so I can close the door and discard my clothes.

"I don't know, he probably left it at a strip club or something." Lydia explains with a snort while I turn the shower on.

"Your dad wouldn't go to a strip club, the man freaks out when a guy on TV takes his shirt off." I deadpan, reaching out to put my hand under the water so I can test the temperature. It's still a bit chilly so I hold off on hanging up on Lydia.

"It was a joke. Are you in the shower?" She demands and I sigh.

"No, if I was in the shower I wouldn't be on the phone with you. I'm just getting ready to take a shower." I explain.

"Alright, well, I'm going to get going. I'll talk to you later, and don't forget to pick me up." She adds before the line goes dead and I sigh. I get into the shower, allowing the scalding water to cascade down my body and relax my muscles before I begin to wash my hair then body.

I quickly get out of the shower, knowing I don't have much time left to get to school since I'm picking up Lydia. I put on my clothes, and wipe the condensation from the mirror so I can attempt to fix my unruly golden blond curls. I eventually give up on attempting to fix the mess and instead go back into my room to grab everything I'll need today.

I get into my car, allowing myself to marvel slightly at the beautiful beast. I have to admit, the car was by far the best surprise my parents have ever given me. This car is far better than my first car; my first car was a rusted Ford something that my parents got at a junk yard for less than five hundred dollars. They made me fix it, since it wouldn't actually run right in the first place. I had to rebuild the whole engine from scratch, alone. But I admit, it was pretty fun and I still kind of miss my old car.

Those thoughts are soon dismissed though when I park in front of Lydia's house. She's already halfway to my car before I'm even in park and she slides into the passengers seat not a minute later, shuddering. I arch a brow at that while I pull away from the curb, heading to school.

"What happened this time?" I question, knowing her parents probably said something to her, explaining why she shuddered, something she only does when she's nervous or anxious. I find the reaction quite odd, though I'd never admit that to her or she'd probably murder me.

"I have to shadow my mom, and she works in a dusty old law firm that specializes in zoning laws. Plus, she wasn't exactly happy to find out I had to go with her to work for a month." She explains with a roll of her eyes and a snort. Though I know that's just a show to cover up her obvious hurt knowing her mom is embarrassed of her.

"That sucks, at least you don't have to shadow your dad though." I add optimistically because her dad is far worse than her mom. Far more embarrassed of her. Plus, her dad works in a factory that makes envelopes so it wouldn't be much more fun than a law firm.

"That's true, at least Mom can stand to stay in the same room as me." She mutters, obviously trying to make a joke but her tone is bitter.

"Lydia," I start but she waves her hand in an attempt to shush me.

"Don't worry about it, I don't care, really." She assures, though it's an obvious lie. I decide not to push the subject though and instead put the car in drive so I can begin to drive to school. The drive is full of silence, the only thing filling it is the soft music of Red Hot Chili Peppers playing through the speakers softly. When we get to school Lydia immediately leaves the car, leaving me alone to gather my things and get out of the car. I walk to my first period class, hoping the day will end soon as I slide into my usual seat.

By the time the lunch bell goes off I'm already drained, ready for the day to be over. I go into the cafeteria alone, silently wondering if Lydia is still in a foul mood. I get some donuts and coffee from the lunch line, before I begin the walk towards my car.

I eat in the car, knowing I probably won't get the chance at my mom's work and if I don't leave now I won't make it to Mom's work in time. I finish my food and start driving towards her work, dreading the next month. I don't exactly feel like spending the next month at a clothing design business, that's going to be so boring.

Nonetheless I continue the drive, parking in the large, empty parking lot where the office is. I kill the engine and reluctantly slide out of my car, scanning the parking lot. There's only two other cars here, one of them being my mom's small blue Impala. I walk towards the three story building, wondering which story my mom's company is on. When I get closer to the front doors, however, I realize the entire building is the company.

I walk through the double doors, shivering slightly at the chill in the office and immediately walk up the what seems to be the receptionist desk. The woman sitting behind the dark red wood desk—with perfectly styled red hair, bright green eyes, too much makeup, and a tight black cocktail dress—glances up at me in boredom.

"May I help you?" she all but sneers, most likely irritated that I interrupted her time on what looks like Facebook on her iMac computer. Nonetheless I smile at her, wanting to make a good first impression so I won't have to deal with her being a bitch the whole month.

"Actually, I'm Levy Newark. My mom--"

"Oh! Of course, Mrs. Newark told us her son would be here for the next month. I just didn't realize you would look so, casual." She adds, still a bit of a rude tone to her voice as if she feels superior to me. I understand why she says this though, she expected me to wear suite and look like one of those old guys who hate their jobs. I feel my eyes twitch at that, my irritation at her beginning to become stronger than my intent in staying calm. However, before I can blow up at her for being so irritating, a voice interrupts us.

"Julie, stop talking to Mr. Newark and do your job or I'll allow you to be fired, get it?" the voice nearly growls. The woman, Julie, nods meekly and begins furiously typing on her computer, her entire face turning red with embarrassment. I turn to face the owner of the strong voice, and I feel my breath catch in my throat.

The man in front of me has golden brown hair of silk, black eyeliner around his gorgeous dark golden-like eyes. A sleeve of intricate ink drawings of Celtic designs flowing through numerous black flowers cover both his arms and disappear under his short sleeved V-neck shirt. The permanent black ink covers not only his arms, but also the top of his hands, and I suspect on his chest also considering I can see the same soft ink peeking out from under the visible part of his chest.

"Hello, you must by Levy Newark, your mother mentioned you would be here for the month. I'm Jeremiah Cole, but you can call me Jer if you'd like." The man greets, extending his hand towards me. I shake his hand, attempting to come up with something, anything, to say.

"Um, yeah." I clear my throat, embarrassed that I couldn't find anything better to say.

"Come on, Levy, your mother works over here." He explains and as he begins walking away I follow. I admire the way his body moves, and I speak before I can even realize what I'm saying.

"I actually have to observe all the workers, which is why I have thirty days to do this. So I have to observe you all work." I blurt out, coughing awkwardly. He turns to me and smiles softly.

"Okay, well let's go see your mother and she can go ahead and explain everything from there." He explains and I nod in agreement as I trail behind him once more.

"Oh, Levy!" I look up in surprise to see my mother stand from her previous position in front of her desk. "I thought you would get lost, would you like to sit down?" She asks me, pointing towards a chair behind an empty desk. I glance at Jeremiah in slight interest, deciding I'd rather get to know him better.

"Actually, I'm supposed to observe all the workers. How many workers are there?" I ask in confusion because so far I only count three including my mom. She looks at me in confusion as if what I just asked was stupid.

"Oh Hon, I thought you knew it was only me, Jer, and Julie." She explains and I stare at her in surprise.

"Wait what?" I question. That means I'll have to spend most of my time with Jeremiah, since Julie seems to be unimportant to this company as she only greets people. Well, this will be a fun month.

Chapter Three

- -

{ Chapter Three}

It's been a week since I first started shadowing my mom. Of course, like the little weirdo I am, I spent the entire week with my mother, vehemently avoiding Jer. It's not that I don't like Jer, because I definitely don't not like him. I just don't want to be alone with him when just hearing his name gives me a strange chill.

But this week is different. As it was painfully pointed out to me by my mother, I need to shadow Jer, so I can actually do well on the project. I wanted to crawl in a hole when she told me that but instead I mumbled a 'yeah, sure' and hoped she wouldn't bring it up again, which she hasn't.

I push those thoughts away quickly though and instead focus on where I'm going. I just finished dropping Lydia off at her mom's work, so I'm heading to my own mother's work. The drive is silent save for the light hum of my beautiful engine and the soft music playing from my speakers. Though, while driving I can't stop my thoughts from turning to Jer.

When I first met him a week ago, I did actually consider getting to know him better, but for some reason the thought of being alone with the man scared me more than the full quadratic formula. Though, at the same time I can't help but want to spend time with Jer.

These have been my conflicting thoughts for the past week.

I want to get to know Jer, but at the same time, I want to avoid all interactions I possibly can. And every time I decide to do one thing I end up deciding to do something different.

I sigh and park in what has become my usual parking spot under a tree close to the building. I get out, lock my car, and trudge up the stone walkway towards the large building. I walk into the warm lobby, ignoring Julie who still has yet to warm up to me, and head straight towards my mom's office. When I get there though, I realize she isn't alone. Jer is leaning against a wall behind my mom, talking animatedly about what sounds like a deal to get a new shipment to a large department store.

Even though my mom isn't looking at him, Jer is gesturing with his hands. His eyes are bright and his lips are moving a million miles a minute while he attempts to explain everything. Meanwhile, my mom simply nods and makes a small comment here or there while typing quickly on her computer.

I can't help but feel like a creep, standing just behind a wall to watch Jer. But it's impossible not to watch him. He's so, interesting. And he is obviously enjoying what he's talking about. Though, as I begin to listen I realize the topic has shifted to something that isn't work related so I decide now would be a good time to make my presence known.

I step away from the wall and act as if I just got there, hoping they don't question me. I clear my throat as I walk into my mom's office and both my mother and Jer jump in surprise before their eyes land on me. I clear my throat once more, fidgeting a bit with both their eyes on me.

"I'm here," I state dumbly for lack of anything else to say. My mom looks amused by my redundant proclamation but doesn't comment on it.

"Oh good, I was just talking to Jer about the new shipment we just received. It's our new line of Fall attire. You can stick with him today since I'm busy fixing up the website right now, which would definitely bore you. If that's alright with Jer, of course." She explains brightly, motioning behind her at Jer who hasn't moved from his position other than when his head turned to face me. I try to think of a quick excuse to get out of it, but before I can open my mouth, let alone grasp at a good excuse not to be with Jer, he speaks.

"Of course, I'd love to get to know you better. Come on," Jer replies, smiling a brilliant white smile as he finally pushes off the wall and walks past me, obviously assuming I'll follow. I do, of course, but only because I know my mom doesn't want to deal with me right now. It's not that she's mad at me, but I know she's in the zone and is probably tired of spending hours on end answering all my pointless questions while she attempts to work.

I trail behind Jer at a safe distance, examining his clothing choices today. He's wearing a black undershirt that define his muscles well and show off his tattoos, with a pair of torn jeans, a black watch, numerous different rings, and black sneakers. I avert my eyes from his body though, deciding to keep my eyes on the floor.

I only take my eyes off the floor when Jer stops in front of a door. I look around in confusion, wondering where we are since I wasn't actually paying attention. My eyes return the Jer's back, waiting while he opens the door.

He walks into the room, motioning for me to follow, and when I step in I stop dead in my tracks.

I thought I would find a clean, pristine office with a sparse sprinkle of furniture; maybe a desk with a desktop computer, a chair, and possibly a couch or something. What I did not expect was a room full of a mixture of drawings taped to the walls, cut outs of fashion magazines, drawing boards, scattered pieces of random fabric. The room wasn't necessarily a mess, the floor is clean at least, but the walls— that I don't even know the color of due to all the paper concealing it—are covered completely in paper. Though, there are two couches, a sleek steel desk holding an equally sleek computer, and a couple scattered chairs.

"Wow," I mutter under my breath, jumping slightly when the door closes behind me on it's own accord. Jer chuckles, walking over to his computer to type some things in before his eyes fall on me.

"Not what you were expecting?" he questions, pulling his phone out of his pocket only to place it on the desk.

"No, it definitely isn't." I answer truthfully, walking over to a black leather couch. I sit down and watch Jer who opens his mouth to say something but is interrupted by his phone. He gives me an apologetic look before answering his ringing phone.

"Cole Fashion and Design, Jeremiah Cole speaking." He answers professionally, nodding not a moment later before his deep brows knit together in adorable confusion.

"What? Why is that?" Jer questions, seeming to unconsciously tilt his head to the side in further confusion. After a moment he sighs, but nods. "Okay, thank you for informing me, Jane. Please do tell me when they are free again." He adds before hanging up, running a hand through his hair, before his eyes land on me and he grins.

"What?" I ask in confusion, sitting up straighter on the couch while he walks around his desk towards me.

"What would you say to being a model for the day? The models who were supposed to come just canceled for a bigger gig and I need to get some pictures sent into numerous stores for the displays. You're the perfect candidate for our men's line, you don't have any noticeable flaws." He adds, his eyes roaming up and down my body numerous times, making my face involuntarily heat up.

"Uh, I mean, I don't know anything about modeling. And don't you need my parents' consent?" I question. He shrugs, tapping away at his phone for no more than a minute before his eyes return to me.

"Your mom said it's fine. And there's nothing to it, come on." He adds before walking towards a wall. I feel my brows furrow in confusion at that until Jer opens a door that I hadn't noticed before, to a new room. I follow him in, hearing the door close behind me once more, and watch as Jer uses his phone to turn on the lights.

When my eyes adjust to the light I notice numerous boxes with clothes scattered around, though there's also different sections in the room with separate lights that are no doubt meant to be the spaces where the models are supposed to be. Some of the spaces have plain white backdrops, others have the company logo and name, and some are ordinary things such as a park.

"What's this?" I ask, taking in the numerous boxes of clothes. Though it all seems unorganized at first glance, there actually does seem to be some sort of organization to the entire room.

"Storage, and the area where the models work when they don't have their own preferred venue." Jer explains, tapping at his phone a few more times before tossing it onto a nearby pile of what looks like winter coats.

"What size are you?" He questions, walking towards an unopened box. I blink once, twice, then clear my throat as the question seems to register.

"Oh, I don't know." I admit. As embarrassing as it is, my mom buys my clothes. But even when I buy my own clothes, I never bother to check the sizes, I just buy what fits.

"Hm, I figured as much. Strip." He orders and I swear my eyes bulge right out of their sockets at his dismissive, casual tone.

"What?" I squeak, clearing my throat once more. He glances back at me and rolls his eyes.

"Strip down so I can check the size on your jeans and shirt." He replies and I realize he means strip to my boxers, not strip naked. Or at least I hope that's what he means. I nod nonetheless and start by kicking my shoes off and pulling my socks off.

I yank my shirt over my head next, very aware of the fact that Jer is still watching me. I reach down to unbutton and unzip my pants, realizing only at that moment that my fingers are trembling. I roll my eyes at that and pull my jeans off, hoping Jer didn't notice my trembling fingers. I hand Jer my jeans and shirt and he looks at the sizes before tossing the garments away so he can begin his search through the previously unopened boxes.

He pulls out a white button down shirt and gray jeans. He comes towards me, holding the items in his hand but before he hands them to me, his eyes seem to take in my near-nude body. His eyes stop on something just above the waistband of my black boxers, his brows furrowing. He tosses the clothes on a box before he bends down on his haunches in front of me, tracing his fingers over an old scar on my waist. His eyes look up to meet my own and I can't help the mental images filling my mind at his position in front of me.

"Where did this come from?" He questions, seeming to make it more a demand for the answer. I swallow hard, looking away from him while I attempt to control my body.

"I got into an accident when I was younger, it was minor but I was cut pretty deep with a piece of glass. I guess the scar never really went away." I explain. He nods slowly before standing back up, waving his hand as he picks the earlier discarded clothes back up.

"That's fine, it's pretty light so I can have my editor remove it from the pictures. Here, try these on. They should fit but if not I'll get another size." He adds before turning to walk over to a bag. He pulls out an expensive looking camera along with a tripod and a different lens. I pull on the clothes while he sets the camera up, but frown when I realize the pants are too small.

"The jeans are too small." I state, wondering briefly if he heard me at all since he didn't seem to acknowledge that I spoke. But he turns a minute later and grins, walking towards me. He puts his fingers to his lips, eying me quickly before he reaches out to unbutton all the buttons on the shirt I had previously just painstakingly buttoned.

"No, they're completely fine." He replies before pulling me by the wrist towards the area of the room with a black backdrop.

"What am I supposed to do?" I ask as I fidget behind the bright lights. He turns his attention away from his camera before he shrugs.

"I'll tell you if you're doing something wrong, or if I want you to pose a certain way. But honestly, think of it like having sex: just do what feels natural, Lev."

Chapter Four

- -

{ Chapter Four}

"I'll tell you if you're doing something wrong, or if I want you to pose a certain way. But honestly, think of it like having sex: just do what feels natural, Lev."

The words echo in my mind even now, six hours after I left my mom's office. I don't know why I can't get the words out of my head, though I'm sure it has something to do with me nervously blurting out to Jer after he said those words, that I've never had sex. Then his face took on this unreadable expression before he silently began taking the pictures as if I hadn't said anything.

I sigh as I stare up at my ceiling in the dark. I can't help but think about Jer though. Something about him intrigues me, makes me want to spend as much time with him as I possibly can; while at the same time I don't want to spend more time with him because these weird emotions are messing with my head. I groan and turn to bury my face in my pillow, forcing my eyes to shut so hopefully I can get to sleep soon.

~ ~ ~

"What's wrong, Lev?" Lydia immediately asks when I pick her up the following morning. I contemplate lying, though I know she would figure it out if I lied so instead I tell her the truth; the truth I had only discovered earlier this morning while I was getting ready for school.

"I have a crush on...someone." I mutter, not having the guts just yet to say 'I have a crush on my mother's boss', out loud, where it would forever be let out in the world, would be a secret no more.

"Who?" she inquires, practically jumping in her seat at the thought that I have a crush. I sigh, glancing at her quickly at the stop sign.

"You can't tell anyone." I remind. She nods immediately at this. "It's Jeremiah, my mom's boss." I admit quietly, grudgingly.

"Wow," she whistles then continues; "what are you going to do about it?"

"I don't know. What am I supposed to do about it?" I shoot. She shrugs, looking out the window which I've come to learn is what she does when she's thinking. Meanwhile all I can seem to do is drum my fingers against the soft leather steering wheel, trying not to think about Jer. Of course I can't stop thinking about him; I can't help but think about his beautiful golden brown eyes, his dark tattoos, even his clothes are appealing.

"How about we skip today, we can just skip the first half of the day and go have some fun." Lydia offers when we're a few blocks from the school. I glance at her, thinking about this before I shrug, pulling over.

"What are we going to do?" I question and she seems to think about it for a moment before grinning, causing me to wonder if it was a good idea to agree to skip.

"We are totally going to the mall." She states and I shake my head but don't bother arguing. Instead I start my car and head to the mall.

~ ~ ~

"Oh! We have to go to Jay-Vee's. Of course," she adds, bouncing around the mall like an overly excited puppy. I roll my eyes, wishing I hadn't agreed to carry the bags because now I'm stuck holding ten bags for Lydia. The sad thing though is not a single one of them are mine, I haven't bothered to buy anything save for a few meals at the food court.

"Yeah, yeah. Lead the way." I sigh, trying not to feel embarrassed when we walk into the lingerie store. Of course people don't seem to be looking at me, or at least the other woman aren't, I can't say the same for the men. Because every time I catch the eyes of a man I see the sad look of pity cross his features before he trudges over to his wife or girlfriend who squeals excitedly over all the lacy bras, thongs, and all things in between.

"Lev, do you like this?" Lydia questions quite loudly a few feet away, drawing the attention of a few of the other shoppers. I turn my gaze from the strange pair of crotchless panties that were placed on a mannequin to see that Lydia is holding up a lacy blue nightgown. I sigh, feeling my face threaten to heat up but I push it down and merely walk over to Lydia, done looking at the weird underwear on the mannequin.

"I don't know, it's pretty." I offer but obviously that's not what she's look-ing for because she rolls her now-pink eyes. One would think it's strange that she insists on wearing colored contacts, especially because her natural eye color is actually quite pretty, but I guess the shock has long since evaporated.

"Oh you're no help at all." Lydia mutters before a girl our age, possibly older, comes over with a bright smile.

"I'm sorry, I couldn't help but overhear, I just had to say I think that would look beautiful on you." The girl says, her eyes solely on Lydia whose attention is still on the lacy blue fabric in her hand. It makes me wonder if Lydia even heard the nice girl.

"I don't know, you don't think it would be too much?" Lydia questions, turning to look at a mirror with the nightgown held over her body, no doubt wondering what it may look like. The girl shakes her head quickly, but I'm not sure Lydia noticed.

"I think it's perfect. I'm sure your boyfriend will love it when he actually sees you in it." She adds and finally Lydia turns to the girl, her eyes darting between the two of us.

"Boyfriend?" Lydia echos in question. The girl tilts her head to the side slightly, glancing at me.

"Isn't he your boyfriend?" The girl asks and Lydia cracks a smile, looking thoroughly amused.

"Oh no, he's just my friend. We're gay." I swear my heart stops and my eyes bulge out of their sockets at that. It's not that I mind being gay, but I barely just came to terms with the fact that I have weird crush on my mom's boss. I'm not ready to come to terms with actually being gay, let alone tell anyone. Though the girl doesn't seem to care, if anything she actually looks excited. Then I watch her, realizing she hardly spared me a glance, and is watching Lydia.

"Oh," the girl says, biting into her lip a bit. Lydia shrugs and grins, reaching her hand out towards the girl.

"I'm Lydia, this is my friend Levy." Lydia explains and the girl smiles brightly, taking Lydia's hand in her own.

"I'm Victoria Grace. It's a pleasure to meet you, Lydia." She adds, holding onto Lydia's hand a moment too long after her introduction. I don't comment though and instead glance at my phone, attempting to pretend I got a text message.

"Oh, darn, Lydia. I need to go, my mom just sent me a text." I lie and Lydia sighs, looking quite put out by this.

"Oh hey, I could drive you home if you want to stay. I don't have anything else to do today." Victoria explains, hope filling her pretty green eyes. I nearly chuckle at that but instead grin, glancing at Lydia expectantly.

"That would be great, wouldn't it, Lydia?" I prompt and she rolls her eyes at me but smiles at Victoria.

"Yeah, that would be awesome. Go ahead go, Lev, oh and leave the bags with me." She adds. I nod and drop all the bags to the floor before giving her a quick hug. I leave the store, thankful I don't have to be there any longer, and walk towards the exit of the mall. I check the time, realizing I have long since missed not just school but the time I was supposed to spend shadowing my mom. I don't mind though, being out with Lydia and shopping, as grueling as the ordeal was, kept my mind off Jer.

Of course, I don't mind my thoughts turning to Jer, but it's just painful because there is no way I would ever be able to get into a relationship with Jer. For one, he's older than me, by ten years. And then there's the small little problem of him being my mom's boss. I sigh heavily before all the air is knocked out of me as I'm shoved to the ground. I huff and look up but freeze when my eyes land on the person I ran into - Jer.

"Ow," I state pathetically, having nothing better to say as my mind seems to revert back to a child, whipping my mind of any possibly coherent things to say. Jer seems surprised to see me but chuckles and holds his hand out to me, allowing me to get a better look at the thick black cross permanently etched into his flesh.

"I'm sorry, Levy, I didn't see you there." He apologizes while I grab a hold of his warm hand and allow him to help me off the ground.

"It's okay, I mean, I'm fine. I wasn't paying attention." I ramble, dropping his hand when I'm securely back on my feet. His lips twitch with a smile at my ramble but he doesn't comment on it.

"You didn't come to the office today, was the assignment over?" He questions and I avert my eyes from his.

"No, I skipped school with my friend. I had every intention to go today but time sort of got away from me, by the time I checked the time it was already too late." I lie because I didn't have any intention of going to school nor to my mom's work today. He chuckles at this and motions for me to continue where I was going, no doubt planning to follow and talk rather than stand in the middle of the mall to talk. I begin the walk to the exit once more with Jer next to me.

"Don't worry, Levy, you don't have to lie. I understand that you don't want to spend time at the office, I don't mind. Though just a heads up, your mom is a bit mad that you never came." Jer explains with an honest tone and a carefree shrug while we exit the loud, crowded mall. I cringe at that though, unable to help myself from thinking of how mad my mom probably is.

"Damn," I mutter and Jer laughs a bit while we walk through the parking lot.

"I'll say, I feel for you, she is a scary woman when she's mad." Jer adds with a shudder and I sigh, unable to help myself from nodding in agreement.

"I know, she's intimidating." I reply and stop in front of my car. "Well I better go, it was nice running into you." I add, shoving my hand into my pocket to retrieve my car keys. I unlock the car with the remote and walk towards the driver's door when Jer's voice stops me.

"It really was a pleasure running into you, Levy. Good luck with your mom, love." He adds, his lips upturned with a small smile before he turns and walks away. I stare at his retreating figure for what feels like at least five minutes, though I'm sure was no more than a few seconds.

Love? What could he mean by that? Or maybe he just calls everyone love, like when a waitress calls someone hun. That would make sense, except for the fact that I've been around him for nearly two weeks and I've never heard him call anyone love. Then again, I'm probably just over thinking this because of my stupid little crush on him.

I sigh and roll my eyes before I get into my car to drive home, hoping my mom isn't too mad at me when I do arrive home. I don't feel like being chewed out right now, especially because I can't even tell her the real reason I skipped today. The reason that I happened to run into at the mall, and who called me love. Yeah, she definitely can't know, no one can.

Chapter Five

{ Chapter Five}

To say my mom was mad was an understatement, she was furious. She yelled at me for over an hour last night before finally telling me if I ever do something that disrespectful again she will punish me severely. I decided not to find out what she would do to punish me and vowed to never skip a day of this shadowing assignment again.

"Lev?" I snap out of my thoughts and turn to Lydia in question. She rolls her now-black eyes and takes another bite of her burrito.

"Yeah?" I question and she sighs.

"Did you hear a word I said?" She demands and I shrug.

"No," I reply honestly. She rolls her eyes once more before explaining once more.

"I have a date with Victoria tonight since it's Friday. We continued shopping after you left and really hit it off. I think I really like her," Lydia explains honestly and I stop eating in surprise. Oh sure, Lydia has had numerous girlfriends over the years but she never had much interest in them. As horrid as it is, Lydia only dated her exes to get in their pants. She would do anything to have a good time, and anything means anything. So if she says she likes someone, then she really must.

"Really? You don't just want to get down her pants?" I add and Lydia shakes her head in disagreement.

"No, I really like her, Lev. She's so nice, and she gets me. I've never felt like this before, I think she's going to be something serious." She adds, sounding awed by the idea.

"Well that's great, Lydia. I'm so happy for you." I reply with a smile though I can't help the pang of jealousy that runs through me because she gets to date the person she likes; while here I am, if I so much as think of Jer I'm basically committing a crime. I sigh and glance at the time.

"We better get going, we only have a few minutes before we have to leave." I state, secretly happy to have a way to change the subject. She nods in agreement after checking the time and after throwing her trash away she follows me out to my car.

I pull up to Lydia's mom's work not a minute later, allowing Lydia to get out once I park the car. When she gets out I call out to her; "Good luck!" She nods and gives me a thumbs up. I know she'll definitely need it today as she decided to wear black contacts, dye her hair dark red, and wear a short black dress.

When I tried to tell her that she may be pushing it, she merely waved me off so I decided to stay quiet. I remember the last time I tried to give her fashion advice when she wore a nearly transparent white cut off shirt; she told me to shut up then proceeded to slap me for apparently insulting her fashion taste. I didn't try to explain I wasn't insulting her fashion taste, I was merely trying to warn her before a teacher saw the shirt and marked her with a dress code violation. That very thing happened though, and every time she complains about the apparently strict dress code, I can't help but tell her I tried to warn her.

The school really doesn't have a very strict dress code policy. Basically, if a student is fully clothed and is not wearing something overly sexual, the school doesn't care. Honestly, a person has to all but walk around naked, or near naked, to even be written up. So obviously Lydia's shirt was pretty bad.

I shake those thoughts away though when I park in front of the large building under the same tree as I have been doing for nearly two weeks. I walk into the office and just go to Jer's office because that's where I've been frequenting the most the past week. When I walk in Jer glances up in surprise from his desk but seems to smile a bit when he realizes it's me.

"Ah, hello, Levy. Why don't you take a seat, I don't have much to do today so I can just tell you about the processes we go through to get everything in stores." He explains and I nod, taking a seat on the couch. After I do he begins explaining the process while I listen intently, wanting to remember everything so I can start writing the next half of my paper.

~ ~ ~

"I'll see you Monday," my mom says to Jer when we're leaving. He simply nods from his desk, scribbling on a piece of paper so my mom motions for me to follow her so we can leave. I follow her out of the building and glance at her curiously.

"Isn't Jer - emiah, Jeremiah leaving?" I ask curiously, correcting myself before I call him Jer because I'm sure my mom would get mad about being so informal.

"No, he stays at the office pretty late." She explains and I nod in understanding but I can't help the slight pity I feel for him. Does he stay so late because he doesn't have anyone to go home to? It's quite sad actually, but

I decide not to think about it and instead part ways with Mom. I get in my car and head to a local coffee shop to finish my paper.

After I order a coffee I take my laptop out of my bag along with my notes I took throughout the week, and begin writing. I only stop to retrieve my coffee and drink some before I continue writing.

"Um, excuse me," I glance up in surprise, yanking my earbuds out to hear better but I freeze. I'm met with the grayest eyes I have ever seen, to the point that it's actually a bit eerie because his iris nearly blends with the whites of his sclera. His dark brown hair is swept out of his eyes, making him look slightly older.

"Yeah?" I squeak, feeling heat rise to my face as I clear my throat in embarrassment and take a sip of my coffee to make it seem like the heat of it is causing the pink tint of my face.

"I'm sorry, I just had to come over. I saw you when you came in and wanted to talk to you and now I'm going to leave because I'm rambling and embarrassing myself." He says quickly, turning red as he averts his gaze and turns but I laugh a bit.

"Wait, wait. It's okay, why don't you have a seat?" I offer and he turns, looking relieved as he takes a seat in the empty chair across from me. I close my laptop and place my notes on top before I turn my attention back to him.

"I'm Ian Kelly." He says, extending his hand to me. I smile and nod.

"Levy Newark." I reply with a smile and clasp his extended hand to shake it. He nods and glances at my laptop and notes in interest.

"Are you writing a paper?" He questions and I nod, tilting my head to side slightly in confusion.

"Yeah, I am. Do you go to Lincoln?" I ask because I haven't seen him around school, I would definitely remember those eyes if I had run into him.

"Oh, no, I go to the private school a few blocks away. St. Ignatius." He explains with a shrug as if it's not a big deal to be going to a the Harvard of high schools here. I nod, though, tucking that piece of information away for later as something occurs to me. I grin slightly, probably a bit wickedly.

"So do you have to wear uniforms?" He chuckles and his face turns bright red once more. It's weird but I can't help but like his reactions to the simplest of questions.

"Yeah, it's not that bad though." He explains with a shrug. I nod in understanding because although I've never personally had to wear a uniform, I never thought it would be as bad as everyone says it was.

"Are you a senior?" He asks and I nod. "Me too." He adds with a bright smile. It's the kind of smile that makes you want to smile, even if there's no reason to smile. It's nice.

"I may be really wrong, and this is probably sudden. But will you go out with me?" He blurts and I tilt my head.

"On a date?" I confirm and he nods but speaks quickly.

"But I mean if you don't want to, that is completely fine. I just blurt things out when I shouldn't and then I ramble, like I am now. I'm gonna go ahead and shut up because you're looking at me like I'm crazy." He continues, looking mortified and I can't help but laugh.

"It's fine, really." I assure but I don't say if I will go or not. Ian seems really nice and all but I can't help but think about Jer. I still like Jer, that much is obvious but it's also painfully obvious that there is little to no chance of anything happening with Jer. He's older than me, not to mention it would be illegal if anything happened between us. That relationship would be nearly impossible, but I could have a relationship with Ian. It could work, would be safe, legal.

"Okay," I agree at last with a smile and he seems to sigh in relief.

"Oh thank God, I thought you were mad that I asked. I mean, I didn't even know if you were gay and I asked you out. Not that you look gay or something, quite the opposite actually. I mean you don't look straight either, I guess. Oh God." He groans and drops his head in his hands while I laugh.

"It's okay, really. I think that was a compliment anyway." I assure and he sighs in relief once more.

"Wow, thank you. I mean, I can't believe you're even still sitting there. Most people get tired of my rambling but it only happens when I'm nervous, sort of. I mean, I ramble a lot but it gets worse when I'm nervous." He explains quickly and I arch a brow, amused by him.

"So you're nervous right now?" I question and his eyes go wide.

"No, I mean, kind of. I should probably just get your number before you change your mind." He adds. I chuckle and shake my head, scribbling my number on a piece of paper and handing it to him.

"I have to get going, actually. But call me. I'm free all day tomorrow and Sunday." I explain, packing up my things.

"Oh okay, I'll definitely be calling you. Wait, that sounds like I'm desperate. I'm not desperate, I swear. I mean, I've never actually been on a date, or even had a boyfriend. But I'm not desperate. I chose to be single. Oh shit, that makes me sound like a lonely, bitter, forty-year old with a hundred animals. I don't have a hundred animals, I swear, I only have two. Wait, do you like animals?" I laugh more at the look of insistence on his face.

"Ian, it's okay. I love animals, I used to have a dog actually. I'll talk to you later." I assure and he nods, looking relieved. Then I leave the coffee shop, getting in my car to start the short drive home.

Chapter Six

"Levy, dinner is almost done. Where have you been?" Mom asks when I get home and I sigh.

"I was just at the coffee shop so I could work on my paper." I explain honestly when I enter the kitchen but I leave out the meeting of Ian so she doesn't ask any more questions. She turns around from the stove to face me with a disapproving look in her dark green hazel eyes.

"You should have told me what you were doing, or at the very least called to tell me you would be out that long." She continues in obvious irritation and my brows furrow in confusion.

"Why are you getting so mad? I forgot to tell you where I was going, I'm sorry." I add with a small, nervous laugh. She doesn't look overly thrilled, nor does she seem to accept my apology but she does turn back to the stove.

"Dinner is going to be ready in a few minutes, would you go tell your father?" she seems to ask but her voice holds demand. Her odd mood throws me off but I brush it away and leave the kitchen to tell my dad about dinner. I go into the living room where my dad's watching some sort of building show on TV, and sit down on the couch next to him. He glances at me in acknowledgment and bumps my shoulder with his own.

"Hey, kid, haven't seen you in a while." He jokes and I roll my eyes, looking at the TV without watching it. I couldn't possibly say what compelled my next train of thoughts, maybe it was the fact that my dad is admittedly one of my best friends. Whatever it was, I couldn't help but feel compelled to tell my dad that I wasn't straight.

It was a fact that didn't bother me as much as I thought it would. Of course it's a bit unsettling to find out I'm apparently attracted to men after assuming my whole life that I would just marry some bimbo, have a couple kids and get a mediocre, blue-collar job. So realizing that probably won't be happening is a bit of a surprise.

My thoughts are abruptly stopped when Dad mutes the TV though. I glance at him in question while he puts the remote back on the coffee table in front of the couch.

"I feel like you have something to tell me." He explains, turning to face me fully, giving me his full attention. I sigh heavily and meet his eyes directly.

"You can't get mad." I state and he arches a brow in question.

"Are you doing drugs? Drinking? Eh, I won't be mad, you're almost an adult so I trust you to make smart decisions." He replies with a shrug but I see worry in his eyes, no doubt worried that I've done something terrible.

"I'm not doing anything like that, I promise." I assure quickly so he doesn't worry. "I, um..." I scratch the back of my head nervously and clear my throat. "I'm not, uh, straight." I add awkwardly, dropping my gaze to my lap.

"Oh," he says calmly, sounding almost... confused? I glance up at him to see that he does indeed look confused.

"Oh?" I echo in my own confusion.

"I'm sorry, did you expect me to be mad?"

"Well, yeah." I admit and he chuckles, a small bit of hurt in his eyes no doubt from knowing I was scared of his reaction.

"Why would I be mad? It's not like you're doing drugs or something. Besides, now I don't have to worry about you getting someone pregnant." He adds with more laughter and I can't help but sigh in relief.

"Dinner is almost ready." I state, changing the subject because there's no reason to continue talking about it. He nods and we go into the dining room just as Mom puts dinner on the table. We sit down at the table and soon Mom joins us.

The dinner is boring, Dad talks to Mom about work while I continue to eat in boredom. When I finish I excuse myself and go to my room to go to sleep, happy about how the day went. I managed to meet a new guy, a new friend, and my I came out to my dad who took it better than I expected. It was definitely a pretty good day.

~ ~ ~

"Hey, Lydia. Can you come to my locker with me? I forgot my wallet in there." I ask Lydia when we're at lunch the next day. I give her no room to object as I stand and start the walk in the direction of my locker. I hear her heels clicking on the tiled floor behind me seconds later though so I continue until I'm out of the cafeteria. I turn and sigh while Lydia stops in front of me in surprise.

"What are you doing? I thought--"

"I don't need to go to my locker. I wanted to talk to you away from Jess." I explain, interrupting her before she can try to say anything else. She tilts her head to the side in confusion, her eyes wide in curiosity.

"What did you need to talk about?" she questions curiously. I sigh and tell her about Ian, then about my idea to date him in order to get over Jer because there is no way I can be with Jer; it's impractical. She seems to think about all that I said as she bites her lip in concentration.

"You should just forget about Jer. Like you said, the relationship would be near impossible. Besides, this Ian sounds interesting, what with being in private school. So just go out with Ian and if you like him then you can just forget all about Jer." She explains and I nod in agreement. I can't deny that I still have odd feelings for Jer but it's obvious the relationship would be platonic. So why should I torture myself with thoughts of him when there's a perfectly good guy out there who obviously likes me?

I sigh and follow Lydia back to the table in the cafeteria. We both sit down and I ignore Jess's questioning glances, instead I focus on finishing the outline for the paper that I forgot to do before beginning to write it. I continue catching up on the homework I didn't do for the project for the rest of lunch, only stopping to eat some fruit Lydia offers me.

~ ~ ~

"Levy?" I blink and glance away from my phone to look at my mom.

"Yeah?" she sighs, looking irritated that I wasn't listening to whatever she was saying about her job. For some reason today she insisted that I spend the time with her to observe her job, her role in helping the company strive and all that. I agreed because I know what she does already, Jer explained it at one point so I knew I could easily just relax. Or so I thought.

"You're not paying attention. Who are you talking to anyway?" she demands and I arch a brow.

"A friend." I reply in confusion. Why in the world does she care who I'm talking to anyway.

"What friend?" she prompts. I straighten in my chair and tilt my head to the side, still completely confused.

"Why do you want to know?" I ask but immediately regret it because her brows furrow and she straightens, obviously trying to look more authoritative.

"Leviathan, I am your mother. When I ask a question, you answer it. So who are you talking to?" she nearly grounds out between clenched teeth. I shift uncomfortably, not used to my mom getting mad at me. My parents are both quite laid back so when they get mad, it usually means I did something wrong. Only, I have no idea what I did wrong this time. I've asked my parents why they've asked me questions before and they never get mad.

"It's Jessica." I lie, not wanting to explain to her about Ian. She seems to relax significantly at the response and even smiles.

"Okay, thank you." She turns back to her computer and starts typing furiously for a few minutes before stopping once more.

"I always liked Jessica, she's a nice young woman." She adds while I resist the urge to snort. Jess is nice, sure, but not in the way Mom means. She doesn't realize that Jess frequents numerous twenty-one and over bars around town, she also smokes pot with her older brother, and I'm pretty sure she's slept with most of the football players at school. She's anything but a nice young woman, but I don't bother to tell this to Mom as she would no doubt be mad about it.

"Sure," I reply in agreement instead before I get back to messaging Ian.

Ian: *So, now that we know each other a bit more. Do u wanna go out 2nite?*

Out? As in on a date?

Ian: *dunno, u want it 2 be a date?*

I think about it for a minute, my fingers hovering over my phone's bright screen. I know I told Lydia that I wanted to go out with Ian in order to forget about Jer, but what if I don't get over Jer? What if I just hurt Ian by basically using him? Maybe I should just be his friend.

However, even with these thoughts my fingers seem to have a mind of their own because before I know it I've sent Ian a message agreeing to go out with him. I thankfully don't have time to curse myself for that though, because he replies not a minute later with the time to be ready and where to meet. I smile to myself, already happy that I decided to go out with him. Who knows, maybe I'll be able to get over this stupid crush on Jer.

Chapter Seven

{ Chapter Seven}

"Where are you going?" Mom demands when I head to the door after getting ready for the date. I glance at her over my shoulder and shrug.

"I'm going out with Lydia." I reply smoothly and she sighs, seeming ready to say something until Dad stops her.

"Oh, Hun, let him go have fun. In fact, here's a few dollars for you kids to spend. Have fun." He adds, handing me way more than a few dollars before smiling and shooing me off. I nearly sigh in relief when I get in my car, thankful that my dad intervened before she asked too many questions.

Before I drive off, I send a quick text to Lydia, telling her to say I'm there if my mom calls for some reason. She replies with a questioning "okay" and with that I drive to the location Ian said to meet him.

The place Ian said to meet him is a restaurant. It's more like a diner however, with the exception of the food being more of pasta, soups, and bread bowls rather than burgers.

I park my car on the side and after I assure the alarm is on I walk into the restaurant. I walk past a guy who is obviously in a gang, making me walk past quicker and wish my car wasn't worth so much. I push those thoughts away though because I know I saw a nicer car in the parking lot, and walk to the back where the familiar eerie gray eyes catch my own hazel eyes.

Ian smiles brightly when I get to the table and stands, looking like he wants to hug me but instead holds his hand out. "Hey, you made it."

I arc a brow, shaking his hand a bit awkwardly. "Did you expect me to stand you up?"

"Maybe," he replies and I sit down, ignoring his words. We both look around, the awkward air trying to set in because we obviously don't know what to talk about.

"Can I get you a drink?" The waitress seems to come out of nowhere and I nearly jump in surprise. I glance at her and then look back at the table.

"Just a water, please." I reply and she nods before her bright blue eyes look to Ian. He glances up in surprise, looking at her as he seems to realize only now that she's talking to him.

"Oh just water for me too, thank you." He replies quickly and she nods with a smile before leaving. He glances at the table before opening a menu and I nearly chuckle at his obvious awkwardness.

"Have you been here before?" I ask, looking at my own menu. His head snaps up in surprise.

"Wait, me? I mean, oh yeah, of course you're talking to me. Oh uh, yeah my parents and I used to come here all the time. It's pretty good, I don't like the shrimp though but I'll go ahead and shut up now..." He rambles and I chuckle, thoroughly amused with his rambling.

"Used to? Why did your family stop coming?" I wonder aloud, tilting my head to the side in confusion. He shrugs, looking at his menu once more.

"Oh, my mom died, so my dad doesn't want to come here anymore since it reminds him of her. I mean, he got remarried but he still misses my mom, you know. So he doesn't like being here." He explains rapidly and guilt fills me immediately.

"Oh God, Ian, I'm so sorry, I had no idea." I apologize immediately, feeling horrible for asking him that.

"It's okay, she passed away a little more than ten years ago. I mean, I miss her but it doesn't bother me as much as it used to. I mean, when it first happened I was a wreck, I was only seven of course but still. My dad was great though, he helped me get over it. But you know, I still miss her." He explains rapidly and my brows furrow in concern. I reach over and place my hand on top of his in comfort.

"I'm sorry." I state honestly. I know it won't do anything, but hopefully it helps some. He grins, seeming to let his mood change in a blink.

"It's okay, Levy, really. Anyway, what are you getting? I'm getting the chicken soup, it sounds great right now. It's really good. I also like the chicken salad, they have good chicken. I love their chicken." He continues and I smile a bit, happy that I didn't kill the mood completely.

"Okay, I'll keep that in mind." I reply with a new round of chuckles while I scan my menu once more. I decide on a chef salad and we both order once the waitress comes back with our drinks.

"So, what were you writing at the coffee shop?" He questions and I realize that despite the fact that I told him I was writing a paper, I didn't actually tell him what it was about. So I explain the entire project to him, leaving out my weird crush for Jer, and what the paper is about. He seems to hang on my every word and continues to listen intently, not seeming to zone out or stop listening at any point.

"That's pretty interesting. The most interesting project I did was on snakes, they're pretty interesting but not that interesting. I liked doing it, but it wasn't all that big, just write a small summary about them and make a PowerPoint, which was the hardest part because I didn't know how to work the computer. Imagine my embarrassment when my dad had to help me work technology. It took him nearly three hours to teach me how to use my phone. And I'm way off topic, and rambling, again." He explains quickly before blushing lightly and I chuckle, amused by him. His rambling isn't just amusing though, it's actually kind of adorable.

I can't help but watch him for a few moments, no longer than a minute, but it still makes me realize that I definitely like him more than a friend. And perhaps he's the right choice, the one I need to be with. The safe option.

"This is nice." I state, smiling as I make my final decision; I reach over and lace our fingers together, both hoping and knowing I made the right decision. He seems to relax, a strange sort of adoration entering his beautiful gray eyes.

"I'm glad you're enjoying yourself." He replies as the food arrives. I take my hand back to eat but I can still feel the warmth of his hand in mine. It felt nice, normal.

We continue to eat and talk casually after that, the conversation flowing nicely. Ian does have his moments of rambling from nervousness but I find it quite adorable and entertaining.

"I'll pay," I state once we're finished with our meals and have gotten the check. He gives me a look that says he wants to object, he really wants to, but I already have the money my dad gave me out and I put half of it in the small black tab. He looks only slightly irritated but I ignore him and follow him outside.

"This was nice," I repeat once more when we're outside in the cold winter weather.

"Actually, could we walk?" He questions and I glance at him before shrugging.

"Sure." I follow him down the road, past shops displaying a wide range of merchandise including jewelry, clothes, and even lingerie in an adult store.

I shiver at one point though, realizing only now that I didn't grab my jacket, and I'm wearing a short sleeved shirt. I mentally roll my eyes at my stupidity, I should have remembered that it was this cold outside. Before I can finish my thoughts, however, a warm, heavy object is placed over my shoulders and I realize it's a jacket. Ian's jacket.

"Ian, you don't have to give me your jacket. I'm perfectly fine without one, it's not that cold. Besides, now you'll be cold." I add in a scolding tone but he shrugs.

"It's okay, I can handle a little cold, I can't handle seeing you cold though. Accept the gift graciously, Levy." He replies with a lopsided grin and I sigh, not bothering to argue. I glance around the area with a small smile, remembering when my dad would take me to this side of town for ice cream and toys.

Then as I got older the toys became books, however we still got ice cream. It's those memories though that make me miss my childhood. It was so fun, relaxing. And now I'm nearly an adult, a man who has to make smart choices, I can't be that kid who would beg his dad for extra sprinkles on his ice cream, or another book even though I already have hundreds. I have to be responsible, I have to make wise decisions.

And when I glance back at Ian who seems also lost in his own world, I realize I'm making a good, wise choice. I sigh and wrap the jacket tighter around me momentarily, my senses being assaulted with the smoky scent that is Ian.

"Ian," I call, stopping and waiting for him to stop. He stops and turns in confusion, standing in front of me, nearly the same height as me, with his head tilted to the side in confusion.

"What's wrong?" he asks immediately, looking incredibly worried that something may be wrong. I shake my head and smile, glancing around the deserted street. I reach my hand up to brush against his jaw before I lean forward and kiss him lightly on the lips.

His lips are a bit chapped, but that doesn't seem to bother me as I continue to kiss him, licking his bottom lip lightly before I pull back. I attempt to catch my breath despite the fact that the kiss was so short so I shouldn't be out of breath. He seems surprised, incredibly surprised, but there's a smile gracing his pink lips.

"What does this mean?" he questions, one of his arms still wrapped around my waist while his other is cupping my chin, stroking my cheek.

"It means the date went really well, and I want to see where this goes." I reply, tracing my finger over his chin to his bottom lip. I catch it with my finger, pulling it down lightly before I lean forward, giving into the temptation to kiss him once more.

"Could this go to more than friends?" he shoots and I chuckle, dropping my hand.

"Ian, we were more than friends the moment we met." I state with another round of small chuckles.

"Good," he whispers and I smile. While I look into his light gray eyes, I can't help but realize I haven't felt this happy, this comfortable with any of my previous girlfriends. It never felt this way, and I love the way I feel. Sure, I still can't get Jer completely out of my head, but Ian will make me forget him; he has to.

Chapter Eight

{ Chapter Eight}

By the time I get home after talking a bit more with Ian, it had begun to rain. So when I come into the house, soaking wet, shivering, and yet somehow still reeling from the past hour or so, it isn't a surprise that my mom comes to interrogate me. While I take my jacket, heavy with the fresh rain, my mom makes her way over to me with an unreadable expression.

"How was your date?" I blink in confusion, panic rushing through me so fast it makes my heart skip a beat.

"Date? It wasn't a date," I add quickly, only now realizing how defensive that sounded. She arches a perfectly sculpted brow in a silent question, staring at me for the longest time, as if reading my inner most thoughts.

"I know that. How was the outing? Is that any better?" She corrects in amusement, seeming to make a joke out of it. I blink in confusion, remembering how not three hours ago she was interrogating me about leaving the house, now all of a sudden she's joking with me? I furrow my brows, taking a step back to assess my mom, making sure it's her. When I confirm this is indeed my mom I decide to wave her mood swings off as being her time of the month, that would explain a lot.

"It was good, Mom. But I have to get to bed now. Um, goodnight." I mumble, nearly saying 'goodbye' rather than the simple goodnight. How awkward that would have been. I shake my head and go up to my room, locking my door out of sheer habit.

I discard my clothes until I'm left in nothing but my boxers. I yawn and turn my light off after plugging my phone in and starting my music. I maneuver through my darkened room, slowly adjusting to the darkness while I get comfortable between my large comforter and sheets. I close my eyes, willing myself to think of Ian, just Ian, while I slip into sleep's coaxing arms.

~ ~ ~

"I'm on the highway to hell! On the highway to hell, highway to hell!" I groan and pick up my phone to shut my music off, not wanting to deal with school. I don't mind it but I didn't exactly get much sleep last night. Plus I don't want to go into my mom's work today, I don't want to see Jer. Or rather, I don't want to break my resolve of getting over him. Though, of course I can't just avoid him.

What am I supposed to tell my mom if I did that? *I'm sorry, Ma, I just don't want to be around your boss because I've started to crush on him and I know it would never work out. You know, the usual. So how about dinner?

I roll my eyes at my thoughts and focus instead on continuing to get ready for school. I pull on a gray shirt and black jeans, slipping on my beat up Vans. I run my fingers through my hair quickly before gathering my things and leaving my room. I grab a granola bar from the kitchen and leave the house quickly.

I lock the front door behind me and slide in my car, pulling out of the driveway once I put my music on. I get to school within a few minutes and park, checking my phone because I know I got a message when I was driving.

From: Ian

Hey... did that sound weird? wait, maybe I should have said hi or hello. Or good morning. Is it a good morning? Oh never mind, ignore me...

I laugh at that and shake my head, loving Ian's rambling.

To: Ian

hahaha, you're fine. My morning is good so far, especially since I got to hear from you :)

I reply before getting out of my car and heading into the school. I get to my locker and after I put my stuff away I look around for Lydia. I don't see her and my phone vibrates in my pocket so I shrug and lean against my locker in wait of her. I pull my phone out and smile when I see a new message from Ian.

From: Ian

oh my god thats adorable. Your so awsome, I mean great, like cool crap, even in texting I ramble

I chuckle, biting my lip as I smile at that.

To: Ian

Don't worry, I don't mind your ramblings, it's cute.

I slide my phone into my pocket after that since I see Lydia walking towards me with a grin spread across her purple colored lips. Today she's wearing short black dress with buckles around it that reaches her knees, some black heels and a pink jacket. She all but bounces up to me while the hem of her black dress bounces with her and the buckles making clunking noises. She seems to be in a very good mood, I note.

"What's up?" I question while we walk towards our classrooms. She shrugs, a blush spreading across her cheeks.

"Victoria officially asked me out. We're dating!" She squeals, bouncing up and down in excitement. I chuckle and nod, patting her on the shoulder.

"That's great, I'm happy for you." I add truthfully. From what I've heard, Victoria is perfect for Lydia. She's so nice and kindhearted, caring. I know she'll be good influence on Lydia, and help her through those rough patches in her life that she doesn't typically talk about.

"Thank you. Oh my god, how are things with Ian? What happened yesterday?" she probes and I shrug nonchalantly as though nothing big happened. Of course, a kiss is not exactly big per say, but the fact that Ian agreed to date is pretty important.

"We kissed-" before I can finish she squeals in glee, interrupting me.

"Are you dating?" she demands and I chuckle, shaking my head at her slightly uncharacteristic excitement.

"Yes, we agreed to date." I confirm and she stops to throw her arms around me in a hug. I laugh at that and pull away gently, forcing her to continue walking towards our classrooms.

"That's so great, now you can get over Jeremiah. I mean, obviously there was no way that would happen." She adds and although I know she's right it still stings. I may be dating Ian but there's no denying that I still have that weird crush on Jer. Of course she's right, it would never have happened, but hearing it and thinking it are two different things. Hearing that something you want is implausible is much worse than thinking it. However, I shove those thoughts away quickly and shrug instead.

"I know. Well, hey, I'm going to get to class. I'll see you later." I reply with a smile and she nods, bouncing off to her own class. I walk into the room, going straight to my seat and ignore the loud chatter of the other students. I pull my phone out of my pocket, smiling slightly when I see a new message from Ian.

From: Ian

hm, so im cute? Good to know.

To: Ian

Definitely cute. Hey, can you go off campus for lunch?

From: Ian

i can, y?

To: Ian

I was hoping you could join me for lunch today, over at the new dinner they opened on Birch.

From: Ian

of course, i won't pass up the opportunity to have lunch wt u, or to spend time with u

I smile at that and text him once more but I don't get a reply so I assume he's busy paying attention in class, unlike me. I put my phone away and watch the teacher as he explains that Huxley seems to have made numerous predictions about the future without seeming to realize it in his book Brave New World. I zone out though since I've already heard all about it and already read the book years ago.

I sigh in relief when the bell finally rings for lunch. I leave my class and head to the cafeteria so I can tell Lydia and Jess that I won't be joining them for lunch. I push through the crowd of students trying to get to their own destinations and finally break away from the huge crowd when I enter the cafeteria. I spot Jess and Lydia immediately so I head over there. They both look up when I clear my throat but stay standing.

"I'm going off campus for lunch. I'll see you both later. Oh, Lydia, did you need a ride to your mom's work?" I ask, realizing she may not have a ride yet. She shakes her head with a big grin.

"Victoria is going to drive me, she's picking me up in a bit so we can have lunch first." She replies and Jess sighs dramatically.

"You're both leaving me? How rude." She tosses her long hair over her shoulder and I roll my eyes.

"Oh shush. I'll see you guys later." I add before making my way out of school. I get in my car and drive to the diner.

It's not too far from the school, only about three miles. It's a nice, but small, little family owned dinner. The building was previously a boutique so it has display windows in the front that hold numerous odds and ends including street signs, coins, and even an old mailbox.

I walk into the building after parking my car in the parking lot on the side and texting Ian to make sure he was here. My stomach growls when I enter and smell all the food that's being cooked, while I simply ignore in order to find Ian.

I scan the restaurant and catch sight of the head of brown hair belonging to the boy sitting alone at a booth. I smile and make my way towards the booth, taking a seat across Ian. He seems startled by my sudden appearance but shakes it off and smiles brightly.

"You made it. I mean, not that I didn't think you'd make it. I knew you would. I mean, I didn't, I'm not psychic. I was hoping you would though. But I know accidents happen, that would have been terrible if you had gotten into an accident." He adds, biting his lip before stirring his straw around in his glass of water. I smile reassuringly, noticing that there's another glass of water on the table.

"I'm glad to know you would be upset if I got into an accident." I reply in amusement, taking a sip of the water from the extra glass.

"Of course I'd be upset. I mean, I don't know if it's obvious or not but I do care a lot about you. I haven't known you long of course, but I still care. Oh hell, I sound sappy." He sighs, blushing crimson while I attempt to contain my laughter.

"I like sappy." I assure and his interesting gray eyes catch my own, seeming to search for any hint of dishonesty, which he won't find. He drops his eyes back to his cup and I tilt my head to the side in curiosity. The way he acts, not necessarily timid, but surprised when I say things like that, makes me wonder about any of his past relationships. I want to ask him if he's been in any other relationship and how they were; however I'm interrupted by a waitress to take our order so I save the question for later.

Once we order we continue talking about random things from the weather to politics; and things as trivial as what kind of air freshener smells the best. It's fun, and I find myself smiling the whole time, having a great time. I sigh though when I get a glance at the time, wishing time wouldn't move so fast when I'm having a good time.

"Well, I have to head over to my mom's work now or I'll be late." I state, sad that I have to leave Ian. He smiles though in understanding and after dropping some money on the table - receiving an eye roll from me - he walks me to my car.

"I'll talk to you later. I mean, we will talk, right? Oh but you don't have to talk, I don't mind. As long as you reply. If we're texting of course. But you don't have to text me either. It's your choice." He adds and I chuckle as I always do when he gets this nervous and rambles.

"I'll text you, Ian, I promise." I add before I wrap my arms around him in a hug and kiss him on the cheek. I pull away and he smiles, a bit nervously while I unlock my car. "I'll talk to you later, Babe." I give into the temptation and kiss him chastely on the lips before I get in the car to leave. Though as I'm driving away I see him smile from my mirror, making my own smile wider.

Chapter Nine

When I arrive at my mom's work, or rather get into the building, my smile drops. Of course it isn't the fact that Jer is lecturing the woman at the front desk - who's name I admittedly have long since forgotten - it's the fact that he isn't wearing anything other than a pair of very revealing tight, leather pants.

I clear my throat quickly, making both Jer and the woman jump in surprise. Jer's gaze snaps to me, looking ready to lecture me until he realizes who I am, then he smiles his stunningly perfect smile.

"Levy, it's nice to see you again. How was your weekend? Do anything fun? Why don't you go up to my office and wait for me, I'll tell you about our marketing techniques." He adds softly but quickly as if he wants me to leave in order to continue lecturing the receptionist. I nod dumbly, not bothering to answer his questions and instead I just go up to his office.

I pull my phone out and see a message from Lydia asking if I'd be willing to go on a double date. I think about it for a moment and tell her I'll have to ask Ian before I message him with the question. It doesn't take him more than a minute to reply with a confirmation so I agree with Lydia and relay all the information to Ian.

After a few more minutes Jer comes in the room, looking as calm as ever. I look away from him, focusing on my phone instead.

"So, uh, why aren't you wearing a shirt?" I question. He glances at me from the other side of the room where he seems to be looking for something under all the paper scattered around.

"One of my models couldn't make it so I stepped in; I just needed to make sure the clothes fit correctly and looked good before I approved the manufacturing and shipment." He explains but I notice he didn't actually answer my question. I don't bother pointing that out though, and instead focus on my phone once more rather than his chest.

I open my new message and smile at Ian's rambling. I find it funny that even while texting he manages to ramble on, it's cute.

"Levy?" I blink and glance away from my phone but immediately regret it. Jer has somehow moved away from the paperwork he was dealing with to stand in front of me, probably to get my attention. From this close I can clearly see his muscles, and the continuation of his tattoos. I can also see the light sprinkle of hair that disappears in his jeans but I quickly avert my eyes back to Jer's so I don't get caught looking.

"Yeah?" I reply, clearing my throat when my voice breaks. Amusement sparkles in his golden eyes, making me question what he finds amusing but I don't ask.

"I was making sure you're paying attention, I have a lot to say about our marketing techniques. Oh, how is the paper coming so far?" he adds and I shrug.

"I have most of the rough draft done, I need to add some more details but I've gotten pretty much everything I need so the paper is almost complete. The rough draft anyway." I add. He nods in understanding and goes over to his desk to sit down.

"That's great," he replies before going into detail about their marketing. I put my phone away and make notes in my notebook for later, knowing I'll need the information eventually. After a few hours, and well over ten pages of notes, it's time to leave so I mumble a quick goodbye to Jer before I leave his office. It still bothers me that he spends so much time at the office, it's kind of sad but I don't over think it and instead walk down the hall to my mom's office.

She's already begun packing up to leave but looks up when I clear my throat. She raises a brow in question when she notices me.

"Do you need something?" she questions curiously but I just shrug.

"No, I wanted to let you know now that I'm going out with friends so I'll be back a bit late. I might stay the night with Lydia," I add because Lydia did mention that. She doesn't seem to think about it and merely shrugs.

"Okay, just call me if you plan to stay at her house." She adds and I nod. I leave her office and walk down the hall towards the front, passing the receptionist. Julie! That's what her name was. I roll my eyes at that and leave the building. I slide into my car and text Lydia to tell her I'll be at the restaurant in a few minutes.

I drive the fifteen minute drive to Ian's house so I can pick him up, but he texts me to tell me his dad wants to meet me. I pause at that, wondering if he'll approve of me. If I'm even ready to meet his dad. I push those thoughts away though because it's just his dad, it's not like he's going to interrogate me and start planning the wedding.

So I sigh, shut my car off and after I gather my courage I get out of the car. I walk through the grass to the front door of the large yellow house and knock of the matching yellow door. I expect it to be Ian's dad opening the door though - thankfully - it's Ian himself. I smile and immediately pull him into a hug.

"Hey," I greet and pull away while he fidgets.

"Hey, um, nice to see you. I mean of course it's nice to see you. I meant it's nice to see you on my doorstep, I think." He coughs and bites his lip, dragging me into the house by my wrist. "I uh, apologize in advance for my dad." He whispers as he continues dragging me through the house.

I take in the plain white walls, mostly holding some family photos and pictures of Ian at different ages. There's a few pieces of cheap art on the walls, but in general the house kind of seems lacking. It doesn't seem like a home but rather a house full of things. We walk through a hall and stop in a large room, obviously the living room.

There isn't much in this room either save for more pictures and art to take room on the walls. A gray couch sits in the middle with a glass coffee table in front of it; a flat screen TV is mounted to the white wall in front of the couch and there's a few random chairs with end tables scattered around the room. And sitting in one of the many chairs is a middle-aged man that I can only assume is Ian's dad.

He has nearly black hair, which means Ian probably got his own dark brown from his mom. Ian does have a lot of the same features as his dad though, like his defined cheekbones and dimples.

The man looks up upon our entrance and I realize Ian also got his shocking light gray eyes from his dad, though his dad's are a bit lighter, which stuns me. He smiles, making his own dimples more pronounced and I relax slightly. Even if the smile is fake, it puts me at ease.

"Hello there, you must be Levy. I've heard so much about you. I'm Haiden Kelly, but feel free to call me Haiden." He says, standing and walking over to shake my hand. Beside me Ian laughs a bit, obviously nervous.

"Haha, yeah. Well this has been fun but Levy's friend is waiting for us so we'll be leaving now." Ian explains quickly, grabbing my wrist to pull me away but his dad merely grabs the back of his shirt.

"Oh come on, Ian. Don't be so eager to leave. So, Levy, tell me about yourself." I open my mouth but Ian groans and interrupts me.

"His name is Levy Newark, he was born in the 90's, can we go?" Ian whines and I chuckle, noticing that he isn't rambling, though he still has that quick pace to his words, making them sound slightly jumbled at times. His dad laughs, his eyes sparkling with amusement. He pats Ian on the back before nodding.

"You can go, calm down. We should have dinner sometime though, I'd love to get better acquainted with Levy." Mr. Kelly explains to him and Ian rolls his eyes.

"Yeah, yeah. Now we're leaving. Come on, Levy." I expect him to pull me out of the room but first he gives his dad a hug. Then he grabs hold of my wrist once more and drags me through the house, passing a doorway that I assume leads to the kitchen. We get in my car and after I put on some music I drive towards the restaurant.

"Your dad is pretty cool." I state but can't help but wonder where his stepmother is, he did say his dad got remarried so you would think she would want to meet me. Or maybe she's at work, that might be. I make a note to ask him about her later.

"He's my dad, dad's aren't cool. But yeah he's pretty cool considering he's a dad. You know, he's great, I love him and all. But enough of the mushy stuff. Where are we going? And who are we going with? Who's your friend? Is she nice?" he asks and I chuckle.

"We're going to a small restaurant. With my friend, Lydia, and she's really nice." I reply honestly and he nods in understanding. It goes silent but it's comfortable with the music. What makes me really smile though is when I feel his hand cover my own on the gear shift. It's an unexpected move from him since he doesn't seem like the type that would make a move like that but I like it.

The rest of the drive is silent save for the music playing in the background. And all through the drive Ian keeps his hand over mine. It's a simple gesture but it keeps the smile on my face the whole time.

I park the car and get out with Ian following suite. I lock my car real quick before walking over to Ian and taking his hand in mine. I notice a small smile twitching at his lips and it makes me happy to know the small gesture is appreciated. We walk through the doors and I immediately spot Lydia. Mainly because her bright blue hair is a bit of a dead giveaway.

I make my way towards her with Ian in tow and slide into the seat in front of her. Ian sits next to me; in front of Victoria. After we order our drinks we all seem to slip into a slightly awkward silence. I glance at the table before I move my eyes to Lydia, silently prompting her to say something, anything.

"So, Ian, tell me about yourself. How old are you? Do you live around here? Have you come out to your parents?" she asks. I don't bother to get mad at her for asking about his parents, mostly because Ian doesn't seem bothered by the questions; partly because she didn't know and she already asked.

"Well, I'm seventeen, I live over on Birch. I came out to my dad when I knew for sure I wasn't straight three years ago." He explains and I open my mouth to change the subject because I know Lydia is going to ask about his mom, I can just see it in her eyes. Unfortunately she speaks before I can even think of a subject change.

"What about your mom?"

"Lydia," I cut in sharply but Ian just waves me off.

"My mom passed away when I was younger so I never got to tell her." He explains with a shrug. The table slips into an awkward silence once more, because how are you even supposed to respond to that? But apparently Lydia knows how to respond because she breaks the silence.

"How many relationships have you been in before you met Levy?" she probes.

"Oh, uh, one." He replies. We all seem to stop to look at him in confused surprise, even Victoria seems surprised, surprised enough to add to the conversation since being silent the past few minutes.

"One? What happened?" she asks, seeming to forget about the napkin she was previously folding into origami as she had already done with two other napkins.

"It ended." Ian replies, his eyes dropping from Victoria's slightly. I notice his body tense slightly after answering, and his fist clenched under the table. It makes me wonder if the relationship ended on a bad note, or if he wasn't over it. Oh hell, of course it ended badly. Why else would he seem so upset if it hadn't ended badly?

"How did it end?" Lydia pipes in but I glare at her.

"Alright, that's enough interrogating my boyfriend. Especially since I haven't gotten to ask Victoria a single question." I add in amusement but truthfully I want to get the attention away from Ian because it's obvious the question bothered him.

"Oh come on," Lydia whines. "I wasn't done asking him questions."

I roll my eyes at that but continue on with questioning Victoria anyway. While I ask her pointless questions, I slip my hand under the table to entwine my finger with Ian's. He relaxes a bit at that and the rest of the dinner consists of the four of us asking each other questions and sharing funny or embarrassing stories.

"And he cried all night, it was hilarious." Lydia finishes telling her story about when I first slept over at her house and then started crying because she didn't have a nightlight.

"Oh that's not that bad, I think all kids go through that phase when they need a light on." Victoria replies and I hang my head because I know what Lydia's going to say next.

"Oh I know, all children go through that phase. But he was almost thirteen." She adds and I can tell Victoria is trying to hide her laughter by finishing the last few bites of her piece of cheesecake. While Ian on the other hand just laughs, not bothering to cover it. I huff as I feel heat rise to my cheeks in embarrassment but I don't mind in all honesty, it's nice that we're all comfortable around each other. I'm also grateful that Ian's past relationship wasn't brought up again.

When the bill comes we split it to avoid us staying there for another ten minutes deciding who gets to pay. After we pay we all walk out together, still laughing at some joke Lydia made. Me and Ian walk the girls over to their car and after we all say goodbye, promising to do this again, we both get in my own car.

"That was nice." Ian comments and I nod in agreement. A silence falls over us as I drive towards the park in the middle of town that I'm sure is deserted by now since it's already eleven. I park and Ian seems to glance around in slight confusion.

"What are we doing?" he asks, not seeming all that bothered about not going home since he called his dad around nine to tell him he'd be home late.

"I want to talk." I reply with a shrug. I get out and when he doesn't follow I go over to his door to open it. He looks up at me with slight fear in his eyes, causing confusion to wash through me.

"Did I do something wrong? I'm sorry if I said something that embarrassed you, I didn't mean to." He adds, looking even more scared by the minute. I furrow my brows in confusion at that, wondering why he's so scared.

"No of course not. Ian I just want to talk, it's okay." I add, smiling reassuringly before I extend my hand for him to take. He hesitantly takes it and after I close the door I lead him through the grass to a bench in front of a fountain. Of course it's not going right now but I couldn't care less about the silent water in the fountain right now.

"What happened with your last relationship?" I finally force myself to ask, turning my gaze from the still fountain to him. He fidgets with the sleeve of his jacket for a minute and I feel bad for asking but I need to know what happened.

"It was nothing. It doesn't matter anymore, it ended, it's over." He adds, not looking at me. I know he's lying though, it's obvious it had a negative effect on him and though I know I should leave it be I have to know what happened.

"Ian," I start and he glances at me. "Please." I reach over and take his hand in mine to comfort him.

"Nothing, he just wasn't...nice." He replies in an uncharacteristic whisper. I want to push the subject but instead I merely nod, knowing he'll tell me the whole story when he's ready. With that thought in mind I stay quiet and let the comfortable silence wash over us once again so we can enjoy a little more time with each other before I take him home.

Chapter Ten

{ Chapter Ten}

I walk Ian to the front door and feel a bit bad for dropping him off home at midnight. Though when he knocks on the door, apparently not having brought his keys, telling me his dad will still be up for another few hours, the guilt eases. As suspected his dad opens the door and smiles brightly at us.

"Hey boys, did you have a good time?" Mr. Kelly asks and Ian nods with a bright smile matching his dad's.

"Yep, it was great. Would it be okay if Levy stayed over? It's so late and I'm sure his parents are probably asleep. So, you know, it would be rude to wake them this late." Ian adds and I roll my eyes. I know he's right about my parents but the fact is, I doubt he's worried about my parents. Though I don't mind because I suspected from some of his messages that he would want me to stay over, which is why I told my mom I would be staying with Lydia overnight when we were having dinner.

"That's fine with me, as long as Levy's parents are okay with it." Mr. Kelly adds and I nod immediately. "That's great. Hey, Ian, why don't you go upstairs and get everything ready in the guest room."

"Oh come on," Ian whines but Mr. Kelly just arcs a brow, challenging Ian to argue anymore. He sighs in defeat and gives me an apologetic glance before nodding. "Just don't twenty-question him." Ian mutters before walking into the house, past his dad.

After a minute or two I hear a door close upstairs in the house and Mr. Kelly nods. He motions for me follow him into the house so I nervously come in and follow him through the hall. He leads me to the kitchen and stops to turn to me. His expression gives nothing away and after a few minutes I begin to fidget uncomfortably. Is he going to lecture me about dating his son? Tell me not to do anything inappropriate tonight? Oh no, is he going to go full on dad-mode and ask me what my intentions with my intentions are with his son?

"Look, I didn't want to say anything in front of Ian in case it brought up any painful memories, but you need to be careful with him. His last relationship lasted three years and it only ended six months ago. I know he's trying to get over it but if you end up hurting him it will devastate him." He explains and I can't help but sigh because that just leaves me with more questions. Questions that I can't keep contained anymore.

"What happened?" I finally force myself to ask and Mr. Kelly sighs.

"It's not really my place to tell." He replies. I open my mouth to continue prodding but he interrupts me. "Though I know Ian won't tell you the full story and you need to know. His last boyfriend was someone he met at some kind of party, they started dancing and after that night they got to know each other. The guy was a year older than Ian and was by chance going to the same school Ian was. So after a while they got to know each other a bit more and began to date." He sighs heavily, slumping his shoulders as if the words weigh heavily on him.

"What happened next?" I urge him to continue.

"It was unnoticeable at first, small things that would lead to bigger things." He continues and I begin to understand what happened, though I let him continue. "The guy was abusing Ian, he forced himself on Ian before he began to mentally and physically abuse him. I didn't know about it until the guy broke up with him after cheating on him." He finishes with pure rage present in his voice. It's so potent that I have to take a step back even though I'm already across the room from him.

"So I'll only say this once: I swear if you hurt him I will hurt you worse." He growls and I nod quickly.

"Of course I won't hurt him." I reply automatically. He doesn't look convinced but doesn't push it and instead just nods.

"Go on up, Ian is probably waiting for you. It's the second door on the right." He adds before turning to open the fridge, obviously signaling that the conversation is over. I don't bother him with anymore questions and instead leave the room to head down the hall until I reach the set of stairs.

I go up and follow his directions into a nearly empty room. There's a plain bed, a dresser and a window. And Ian. I can't even be bothered to greet him, I just go over to the bed where he's sitting and hug him to me tightly.

"Wow, my dad really must have scared you." He muses but I can't bring myself to laugh, I just want to hold him. Even though I doubt I love him, even only knowing him two weeks at most, I can't help but want to hold him until I stop thinking of what he went through because I care very deeply about him. After a few more minutes I pull back and kiss him lightly on his cheek. He tilts his head to the side, an amused smile on his face but I can see the sad understanding in his eyes.

"I'm uh, going to go ahead and let you sleep. I mean, I'd stay, but I'm tired. I mean not tired of you, just in general. It was a long day, the day was great though. I'll just go now." He mumbles but I still see that he's trying too hard, too hard to be the bubbly person he acts like. I don't pester him but instead nod and give him one last hug before he leaves the room, closing the door softly behind him.

I sigh and after I scroll through my phone for a bit, trying to get my mind off of everything Mr. Kelly told me, I finally succumb to sleep's call. I toss my phone on the bedside table and pull the covers up to my neck as I close my eyes to sleep.

I wake up to my phone going off beside me and I sigh. I open my eyes, ignoring the agitating burn and instead reach over to grab my yelping phone. I check it to see it's just a few new messages from my mom asking if everything is okay and when I'll be home. I notice it's only five in the morning and groan because I know I went to bed past midnight. I quickly tell her that I'll be home later in the day before I yawn.

I toss my phone back on the nightstand, hoping that if I don't look at it I can get back to sleep. I close my eyes and hope to get back to sleep because I doubt anyone is up right now. However, half an hour later I still can't sleep so I get out of bed.

I leave the room, trying to recall where Ian's room is. In this hall alone there's five doors and another turn that I assume leads to another hall. I glance at the door directly in front of me, it looks kind of old and beat up, like the room may belong to a teenager. I only hope I'm right as I knock softly. When there's no answer I try the handle, finding it unlocked I push it open and sigh in relief when I see Ian at his computer with headphones in.

I slip into the room and quietly shut the door behind me before I walk over to him. He doesn't seem to notice me until I tap him on the shoulder. He all but jumps out of his skin in surprise, speaking before even figuring out who tapped him.

"I'm not doing anything, I swear!" he whisper yells as he rips his headphones out of his ears and turns to me. Relief floods through his eyes when he sees it's just me, which makes me wonder what he was doing but I don't ask because from what I can tell from his computer screen he just has a word document open.

"You scared me." He states in a sigh, closing his eyes briefly to calm himself.

"I'm sorry, I didn't intend to. I just woke up and couldn't get back to sleep so I figured I might as well come see you as I would be bored otherwise." I explain with a shrug. His lips twitch in a smile and he shakes his head, glancing back at his computer.

"You can go ahead and hang out here, I don't really get much sleep so it'll be fine with me. I have a ton of books if you like to read. Or we could talk." He adds while turning in his chair to better face me. I tilt my head to the side in curiosity, wondering why he can't get much sleep.

"Why do you have trouble sleeping?" I question and take a seat in a pale blue armchair across from him. His eyes dart away from mine and he sighs, looking intently at the floor.

"It's complicated. I just have sleep issues, it started when..." he trails and I understand immediately. I know I don't know the whole story, but I do understand the gist. So I also get what he's saying, he can't sleep because of what happened. It pulls at my heart to know what happened to him, even if it's not the full story, it still makes me sad, even angry, that someone could do something like that to him.

"What are you doing on your computer anyway?" I ask to change the subject and I can tell he knows what I'm doing. He doesn't object though and bites his lip.

"I'm just writing. It's stupid." He replies with a shrug. I tilt my head to the side in disbelief, arching a brow.

"I doubt it's stupid. What are you writing about?" I ask.

"Nothing, it's just a romance. These two guys meet at a college in the sixties and after a party and some drama they find out they have feelings for one another. They try not to let it show but one person finds out and it's a domino effect. It's just a really rough draft though." He explains and I nod with a smile.

"I'm not the big on reading or books but that sounds pretty cool in my opinion." I assure and though he doesn't look convinced he does seem to appreciate my words. We don't say anything for a while, Ian just stares at his lap while I think over the past half hour we spent talking. At last I glance at him, catching his eyes and smile a bit.

"C'mere." I urge and extend my arms. He bites his lip but after clicking a few keys on his computer and closing it he comes over to me. I glance around his room and stand quickly. "Wait, wait." I lick my lips and drag the arm chair the small ways to his window and open the curtain. It's still dark out so I take my seat, making sure to have a good view of the night from the current position of the chair.

"Alright, come here, babe." I motion with my arms and he rolls his eyes but comes over. He sits down on my lap and after getting comfortable his head rests against my shoulder. I smile and kiss his forehead lightly.

"Go to sleep." I whisper and he sighs.

"I don't know," he trails as if uneasy but I don't blame him.

"I'll wake you up in," I glance at the clock on his wall, "an hour." I add.

He still seems reluctant but his eyes close and soon his breathing evens out. His body relaxes into mine and I smile, closing my eyes for a moment to soak in this moment. I sigh in content and begin rubbing circles slowly on his thigh. After half an hour he moans once but he doesn't seem distressed so I let him sleep because I get the feeling he gets little to no sleep. Though after the hour is up, when the sun begins to rise over the mountains, I do as I said I would and wake him up.

"Ian," I murmur softly in his ear, shaking him a bit to wake him. He bites into his lip hard and his body tenses. "No," he moans out and my heart clenches.

"Babe, it's me. Wake up." I coax, pulling his body closer to mine in case he starts to move to escape. Though I don't mind him getting out of my lap, I do know that when I had nightmares as a kid I would flail and hurt my parents. So I don't exactly want to be hit or kicked as it would hurt and I'm sure Ian would feel bad.

"Stop," he gasps out in pain and I bite my lip.

"Ian," I shake him a bit more and his eyes fly open in alarm. He glances back at me and relief goes through his eyes when he registers who I am.

"Oh hey," he mutters, looking away to take in our current position on the armchair. My arms are wrapped around his while he somehow wrapped his legs around mine. An adorable pink blush tints his cheeks that makes me smile.

"How did you sleep?" I question and he yawns with a shrug.

"Good, actually." He replies. I nod and fall silent so we can watch the sun come up over the horizon.

I may not love him, we may just be two kids but right now I can forget all that and enjoy this moment. This moment with someone I like, watching the sun come up as the new day begins.

Chapter Eleven

{ Chapter Eleven}

The fact that it's been nearly a month since I've began this project, leaving me with only a week left of the project, feels weird. It's not the fact that the project is nearly over, it's more the fact that I've been with Ian for what seems like more than a mere two weeks. I feel like I've known him my whole life when in reality it hasn't been more than a month.

"How do you feel about him now?" Lydia questions and I glance at her from my bed in confusion.

"Who?"

"Jer." I sigh, shutting my eyes tightly as I try unsuccessfully to not picture him.

"Lydia," I start in irritation. We had previously agreed not to talk about Jer; if not because talking about him leads to me thinking about him, then because I'm supposed to be getting over him and talking about him only makes that harder.

"I'm sorry, I just want to know. I mean you are with Ian right now so shouldn't you be thinking of him, and not some other guy." I can't say that I don't agree with her, she has a good point.

"I don't know." I reply honestly because as much as I want to stop feeling something for Jer, I can't. I can't just stop, it doesn't work that way. I can only hope to get over him while the time passes.

"Levy," she starts and my eyes dart to her. She looks hesitant to say the next part and drops her eyes. "That's not right." She finishes in a whisper and I sigh in aggravation.

"Do you think I don't know that? Do you think I want these feelings for Jer? Do you think I don't know how unfair this is to Ian?" I demand with anger pulsing through me. I'm not mad at Lydia, I'm mad at myself because she's right. I run a hand down my face before running it through my hair and finally I look at Lydia.

"Look, I need to get my homework done for English. I'll see you later." I state. She looks reluctant to leave but gets off my bed anyway and walks to my bedroom door.

"I'll talk to you later." I nod at that and she leaves without another word. I sigh heavily and slump back in my chair.

After a few minutes I decide to do more work on my paper to get my mind off of everything. So I take out my notebook that I've designated for the notes I've taken at my mom's work. I flip a couple pages into where I left off and after I open the document in my computer I begin to write more of the paper.

~ ~ ~

I sigh at last when I've finished the next part of the paper but then realize I don't have anything else to occupy my time with. I stare at my computer screen for more than ten minutes as I try to think of something to do, other than think. I drum my fingers on my laptop, tapping a few random keys and listening to clicking before I stop to pull my phone out of my pocket.

I unlock it and decide to ask Jess if she wants to hang out, considering Ian is busy with his dad. Though, that only reminds me that I still haven't met Ian's step mom. And he never really talks about her either, it makes me wonder where she is, considering I've been to his house a couple times and haven't seen a single sign of her in the house. I don't get a chance to think any more about it because Jess replies to my message with an agreement and tells me to meet her at the mall.

I roll my eyes with a small sigh at that because I really don't want to go to the mall but I pack my things nonetheless. I grab my wallet and keys before I leave the house, calling out that I'm going out to whoever is home. I slide in my car and after I let it warm up I head to the mall.

"Levy!" Jess yells from across the food court when she sees me. I roll my eyes but go over there, ignoring the numerous sets of eyes following me.

"Jess, you didn't have to shout, I already saw you." I explain, taking in her appearance. She's wearing a short pink dress that compliments her curvy figure with silver heels and her blond hair pulled back in a high ponytail.

"I just wanted to make sure. So why did you want to meet?" she questions and my brows raise in surprise.

"Why do I have to have a motive? I just want to spend time with you. You're my friend." I add. Though my words don't feel true, probably because I just needed to keep my mind off of Ian and Jer. I do have an ulterior motive and it makes me feel bad but I ignore it when Jess grins brightly.

"Oh great. We can go shopping then." She adds and I sigh. I don't bother to argue but instead follow her through the mall, stopping when she stops.

She thankfully just leads me to a couple makeup and jewelry stores before her phone begins to ring.

"Mom, what's up?" she answers immediately. She nods along to the person on the other end before sighing heavily. "Okay, I'll be there in a bit. Love you." She adds before hanging up. She sighs once more and puts down the box of perfume she was looking at before turning to me.

"What was that about?" I ask and she just rolls her eyes.

"My parents are having a dinner with some people and they're dragging me along. I have to get going now though but I'll see you tomorrow at school." She adds before giving me a quick hug and leaving me alone in the perfume shop. I sigh, dropping my head in realization that I'm alone.

I leave the store and while I'm walking I realize this seems to keep happening. I go to the mall, shop with a girl and then end up being alone in the end. I walk through the mall aimlessly before I decide to go back to the food court and get something to eat. I order a burger and sit down at an empty table. I rest my elbows on the sticky table until my order is called and then I eat slowly.

I watch the people around me in little interest. A mom tries to feed her squirming child while attempting to keep her other child in his seat. A couple seems to be ignoring the loud chatter as they have a sickly romantic lunch, staring at each other rather than actually eating. And of course the many fellow lonely people scattered around just eating.

"I'm beginning to think you're following me." A voice muses and I nearly groan. Of course, the one person I don't want to think about is the one I run into.

"Jer, hey, what are you doing here?" I ask. He glances around in amusement as if the answer is obvious.

"I was grabbing something to eat." He replies with a chuckle. He glances down at the empty seat and arcs a brow, silently asking if he can sit so I shrug.

"I mean in the mall." I clarify but he shrugs.

"I needed to buy some more cologne, it's only sold at one of the specialty stores here." He explains. I nod in understanding and go quiet while I wish I could stop my mind from going to bad places. I shouldn't be thinking of Jer, I should think of Ian.

"What about you? What are you doing here?" he returns and I shrug.

"I was with a friend, she had to leave though." I reply. He nods and seems to take in my appearance before tilting a brow.

"What's wrong?" I huff and roll my eyes, dropping my head in my hands.

"Nothing, just teen drama crap." I lie, assuming telling him that he is one of my problems would not be a good idea.

"Oh come on, it's more than that. Even if it's trivial it's obviously bugging you." He adds and I feel his hand grab one of mine. I lift my head to meet his gold eyes and try to ignore the tingles that run through me at his touch.

"It's not important." I mumble but I can't stop looking at his eyes. They're so intense, full of something. It's obvious he wants to know what's bugging me but I can't understand why. Why does he care if something is bugging me? It doesn't make sense.

"Levy," he starts softly and I drop my eyes from his at the intense emotions running through his eyes. Instead I look at his hand on top of mine, the black ink contrasting against his pale hands. I bite my lip hard as I try not to think anymore into this, as I try to keep my mind from wondering how his lips would feel against mine, how it would feel to be in his arms.

No.

I can't think about that. I can't. I have to stop, I have Ian. And Ian is amazing. Yet my brain barely lets me think of him more than a brief second before I meet Jer's eyes once more. He tilts his head to the side as if in confusion, or curiosity.

"What are you thinking? I get the feeling it's distressing." He adds and I groan because although I don't know Jer very well, I not only feel comfortable around him but I also feel the need to tell him everything I'm thinking.

"Nothing." I lie. He looks skeptical as he arcs a brow and I try not to look at his eyes because I know if I do I'll either do something I regret or tell him something that I'll regret.

"Why don't you want to tell me?" he asks instead of probing me about telling him as I thought he would.

"I just don't want to ruin everything." I admit awkwardly, dropping my eyes to the table as I try to keep my thoughts on Ian. Ian, my boyfriend, the person I'm supposed to have these feelings for. Not Jer, my mom's boss.

"Ruin what?" Jer prompts and I sigh heavily before I meet his eyes once more. I realize when I meet his beautiful golden eyes, how small the table is, and how close we are. I swallow hard as I try to push my urges back, try to think of Ian, but it doesn't seem to work as I find myself moving closer to Jer. I don't know if he noticed me moving closer but if he did he obviously had no objection. What I do know, however, is that when my lips connect to his, it felt right.

Chapter Twelve

{ Chapters Twelve}

You know that moment when you do something and can only think of what you're doing in that moment? When all other thoughts fall away and all you can think about is the moment you're in. It's a great feeling, until the moment is over and reality crashes down on you.

"Oh no," I mumble when I pull away from Jer. I can't read his expression but that's the last thing on my mind. I mean, it's just a kiss, it's not like I cheated on Ian but I shouldn't be having these thoughts in the first place. I should be thinking of Ian, not wondering if Jer enjoyed the kiss.

"Oh," Jer hums, understanding flooding in his golden eyes. I still can't tell if he's mad, weirded out, or otherwise and it's beginning to freak me out. The only solace I get is the fact that I won't have to see this man again after another two days, so if he gets mad I won't have to awkwardly stay at my mom's work while he glares at me or something.

"I'm so sorry," I say immediately, worried about his reaction. His expression gives nothing away still and it gets to the point that I just want to demand he tell me what he's feeling.

"It's okay, Levy." He assures and I stare at him in surprise of his calm, almost amused tone.

"What?" I ask, dumbfounded. He laughs a bit and it eases my nerves a bit to hear the loud sound but it confuses me all the same.

"Levy, I knew when I first met you that you felt something towards me, and if I'm being honest I can feel something between us. So it's no surprise to me that you did that, I practically egged you on." He adds with an unconcerned shrug. I don't know how to respond to that, am I supposed to laugh? Tell him it wasn't his fault?

I have no idea how to react, how to respond, and it doesn't help that all I want to do is kiss Jer again. I don't know if he can read my mind or something but he must have understood what I was thinking because a small grin appears on his face and he leans in to peck me on the lips.

"What was that?" I question when he pulls away. He shrugs, his golden eyes twinkling.

"It seemed like you could use it. Plus I kind of enjoy kissing you." He adds with a smirk. I stare at him for God only knows how long before he clears his throat, glancing away from me. "Look, I know this isn't right but maybe when your assignment is over, we can talk sometime like over dinner?" I blink, once, twice, then find myself nodding.

"Uh, sure, that would be nice." I mumble stupidly, giving no thought to Ian, or the fact that this is my mom's boss for that matter.

"Well great, look I have to get going but I'll see you soon. It was nice having lunch with you, Levy." He adds before leaning over to kiss me lightly on the cheek. "I'll see you soon, love."

With that Jer leaves me alone with my thoughts. Thoughts that immediately go to Ian, poor Ian. I can't be with Ian if all I can think about is Jer. It's not fair to either of them if I do that.

The obvious choice would be to dump Ian, considering I know I'll always have stronger feelings for Jer than Ian. But how could I do that to him after learning what his last boyfriend did? If I broke things off with him it would destroy him, and I don't think I could do that to him.

I sigh and leave the mall, deciding I need to talk to Lydia about all this. However, when I text her to ask if I can come over to talk, she doesn't reply. I assume she's either out with Victoria or is in the midst of being lectured by her parents. So rather than go to Lydia's I just drive around for a bit both to think and clear my thoughts.

Eventually I go home in defeat because it is getting late and Lydia still isn't answering any of my messages. I park next to mom's car and go into the house but freeze halfway up the stairs when I hear Mom talking to who I assume is Dad.

"I'm telling you he's hiding something, Greg." Mom hisses at Dad. I stop on the stairs and listen closely, intrigued and a bit scared about what she's talking about.

"Honey, what do you think he's possibly hiding?"

"I don't know!" she cries and I hear her sigh loudly.

"I really doubt he's hiding anything worse than any other teenager hides." Dad assures.

"He is, I know he is. I just don't know what." She continues. Before they can continue talking I loudly make my way up the stairs.

"I'm home!" I call out as I go into my room and close the door. I drop my keys and wallet on my dresser before I change out of my clothes. I turn out the light after noticing the time and get into bed, hoping I can talk to Lydia tomorrow about everything.

~ ~ ~

"Hey," I greet Lydia when she gets in the car during lunch. I didn't have to take her to school today though since her dad's car isn't impounded anymore, so this is the first time I'm talking to her alone. I open my mouth to start talking about the Ian and Jer situation but pause when I notice her less than happy expression, and her lack of contacts, revealing her natural brown eyes.

It's at that moment that I realize two things: one, something obviously happened with her parents because that's the only time she doesn't wear any color contacts; and two, there was no way I was going to tell her about my problem right now.

"What happened?" I demand immediately. She sighs and goes into her explanation.

"I introduced Victoria to my parents yesterday because she wanted to meet them. They seemed to be on their best behavior, until Victoria left and they told me I couldn't see her. I got a bit mad,"

"Lydia," I groan, sighing heavily because I know when she gets mad, she doesn't just get mad. She throws a fit then her parents find some way to punish her or make her feel guilty.

"I know, I know. So they got mad and grounded me after I let slip that I love her." She continues.

"I'm sorry," I reply and glance at her out of the corner of my eye. She's biting her lip and looking out the window but I can tell what she told me bothers her despite the fact that she's going to pretend it doesn't. I know it bothers her that her parents disapprove of her being bisexual, much less in a relationship with a girl. Though I don't push the subject because I know it won't help, it'll probably do more harm than good.

The drive to her mom's work is silent and though I don't mind it I can tell Lydia is relieved when we get to her mom's work. She gets out of the car and I nod at her in a goodbye because I know she doesn't want to talk, not even to say bye.

I go to my own mom's work and park in the usual spot under a large tree. I sigh and get out of the car to head into the building. The receptionist glances at me, seems to attempt to smile as her painted red lips twitch then goes back to her work. If she was actually nice I would feel bad for forgetting her name even after hearing it numerous times throughout the month. I walk past her and go to my mom's office, hoping to spend the day here.

"Oh Levy, good you're here. Jeremiah is in his office, he's going to explain a bit more about the production process." She greets and I want to argue but if I argue she'll get suspicious so instead I just nod and go to his office.

"Levy, it's so great to see you." Jer greets when I reach his office.

"Hey." I reply and go over to his couch to sit down. He doesn't look away from his computer at first so I take the moment to take in his appearance. Today he's only wearing a simple gray t-shirt that shows off his seemingly endless black tattoos around his arms with blue jeans and sneakers. It makes me wonder why he's almost always dressed so casually but I don't need to even wonder because I know. He's dressed casually because he can be, plus I know he's wearing his own clothes since I saw that exact outfit in the catalog I had looked through the other day.

"Okay, so today I'll go ahead and tell you about how we produce our clothes." He starts and I roll my eyes, interrupting him before he can say anything more.

"Please don't, tomorrow is the last day of the assignment and then I'll give my presentation. I already have what I need, and you've told me about production four times now." I add with a laugh. He glances away from his computer screen to look at me in amusement.

"Have I really?" he asks and I nod. He laughs and shakes his head, typing a few more things before shutting his computer down. "I never noticed. Alright, let's talk about you then." I sober up quickly, staring at him in confusion.

"What?" I have to ask for confirmation.

"Well, you already understand everything about the company, so let's just talk. I don't have anything to do today anyway, I could use the entertainment." He adds before getting out of his chair to sit on the couch next to me. I turn to him, still confused as to why he would want to talk about me. Then again, he said he wanted to get to better know me yesterday so I guess that makes sense.

"Okay..." I reply and bite my lip. "What do you want to know?" I ask at last. He seems to think about this as he tilts his head to the side and looks at the plain white ceiling, perhaps the only blank space in the room that isn't covered in drawings, papers or pictures of clothes. "Hm, do your parents know you aren't straight?" he asks finally.

"My dad does." I reply with a shrug and he nods in understanding, not seeming to have to ask about my mom. He probably knows her well enough to know why I'm hesitant to tell her. "What about yours?"

"My what?" he asks in confusion.

"Your parents, do they know?" I clarify because I'm honestly curious. He doesn't talk about his personal life, or really anything other than work.

"Do my parents know you're not straight?" he muses and I roll my eyes in exasperation.

"No, do they know you aren't." I say. He nods in understanding but the look on his face makes it obvious to me that he was only playing dumb so he wouldn't have to answer the question.

"No they don't, I don't talk to them." He explains.

"Oh, I'm sorry to hear that. Why don't you?" I question.

"They just weren't all that supportive when I was trying to build my company, they wanted me to become a lawyer like the rest of the family. They wanted me to get a good job, a wife, a couple kids, and get a mortgage. I knew it was better to disappoint them because I started a clothing line rather than have them disappointed in me because of who I love." He explains with a shrug.

"I'm sorry." I reply and he shrugs once more.

"It's fine, really. I'm over it." He assures with a smile.

After that we just continue to talk casually until it's time for me to leave. I gather my things and stand while Jer does the same.

"I'll see you tomorrow," I say and start to leave but he grabs my arm gently to stop me. I turn to face him but I'm pulled into his arms before I even finish turning. He hugs me quickly before releasing me and taking my hand to place a kiss on top.

"I'll see you tomorrow, love." He replies with a smile. I nod, a smile of my own finding its way on my lips, and then I leave the office.

Chapter Thirteen

"Hey, uh, it's me. I mean me Ian, not like someone named Me... That would be such a weird name though don't you think? Me. I would hate to have to go around and be like, "hey, I'm Me, it's nice to meet you" maybe that would be cool though. I don't know. I'm going to shut up now. Um, call me back when you can, I'd like to spend the day with you. I'll talk to you later, I hope. I mean I'm not trying to assume or anything. I'm gonna shut up now. Bye."

Beep!

I laugh at the message Ian left me while I was in the shower. I love how much he rambles, it's so cute. Immediately though I feel a stab of guilt because not three hours ago I was kissing Jer and barely even thought about Ian. That's not fair to him, I know it's not. He deserves someone who will care about him, just him. Not someone who's constantly thinking about how he wants some other guy.

I sigh and pull on my black shirt before I call Ian. The phone rings three times and I wonder briefly if he's busy but he answers in the middle of the next ring.

"Hey," I greet immediately.

"Hey, I wasn't expecting you to call back so soon. I mean I didn't not expect you to call, I knew you would. But I thought you were busy. I mean, maybe you were ignoring me. I don't know. I wouldn't know though because I'm not like stalking you or something. That would be weird. I'm not weird. I mean, I probably am but I don't intend to be. I'm not weird enough to stalk you. Unless you want me to. But I don't think you would want that. Would you? I mean, who would want someone to stalk them?"

"Ian," I interrupt with a new round of laughter.

"Right, rambling. I'll go ahead and shut up." He adds nervously and I laugh some more before I sober up.

"Well I called to say I'd love to spend some more time with you today." I say.

"Oh, great. I didn't think you would, not that I doubt that you'd want to spend time with me but because I thought maybe you would be busy. You weren't busy though so that's cool." He replies and I nod with a smile on my face.

"It definitely is, so what did you want to do?" I ask in amusement.

"Oh you can just come over and we can find something to do." He says and I shrug even though he obviously can't see it.

"Alright, I'll be there in a few." I hang up and gather my stuff before leaving the house, telling Mom I'm going to be with friends. I get in my car, pull out of the driveway and begin driving towards Ian's house. I fiddle with the radio at a stoplight to find something good to listen to while I drive. I settle on a station playing Fall Out Boy and begin driving when the light turns green.

I park behind a black Acura that I've never seen before. It gives me a pause and I stare at it for a moment before I get out of the car. I briefly wonder if they have a guest or something but I brush it off because I'll find out in a few moments anyway. I get out of the car and walk across the frostbitten lawn, feeling slightly bad for walking on the grass rather than the steps but I doubt they care too much.

When I reach the door I knock twice and wait. And wait. After a few more minutes I raise my hand to knock again in case they didn't hear but Ian answers and I sigh in relief.

"For a minute I thought you might have left or something." I say honestly in greeting. Ian arcs a brow but shrugs a minute later.

"Why would I leave? That wouldn't be very nice. Well anyway, come on in." He ushers me in and I follow him through the warm hall.

"Ian?" I hear Mr. Kelly call out and notice Ian roll his eyes.

"Yeah?"

"Come in here." Ian sighs but leads the way through the hall into the living room. I pause a minute when I realize Mr. Kelly isn't alone. A rather large man, who must be well over six feet tall with bulging muscles everywhere, pitch black hair and bright green eyes is sitting in the couch close to Mr. Kelly. His green eyes look away from his book for a moment to glance at our entrance, but his eyes lock on me for so long I begin to fidget.

"What's up, Dad?" Ian asks. Mr. Kelly grabs an envelope from the table and holds it to Ian.

"This came in the mail today, I forgot to give it to you earlier." Mr. Kelly replies while Ian takes the envelope and scans it before shrugging. He opens his mouth to reply to his father but the stranger interrupts him.

"Who's your friend?" the stranger demands, his voice rough as if he has something stuck in his throat, or maybe he's just a smoker. In any case whoever this man is, he's ten times more intimidating than Mr. Kelly, which is surprising because Mr. Kelly is pretty intimidating himself. Ian seems to realize something and laughs a bit.

"Oh yeah, I forgot you two never met. This is my," he pauses to glance at me hesitantly and I urge him with my eyes to go ahead and continue. "Boyfriend, he's uh my boyfriend Levy. Levy this is my dad Owen." He says and I stare between the three in confusion because I would have sworn Ian said his dad remarried... oh.

I stare at Ian's two dads, realizing something very scary. If I hurt this kid, I'm going to die by the hands of both these men. It was okay when it was just Mr. Kelly, but now there's, well another Mr. Kelly, a more intimidating Mr. Kelly who could squash me like a bug.

"Shit," I mumble under my breath.

"What was that?" The man asks and I clear my throat quickly.

"It's really nice to meet you," I manage to say, still thinking of all the ways these two men will kill me when I hurt their son. I am so screwed. I might as well have my parents plan my funeral now, order the tombstone, and of course I have to make my will.

"Yeah right, you look like you're about to pi--"

"Owen, leave the poor kid alone. Go ahead and go upstairs. Ah, but keep the door open." Mr. Kelly, er, uh the less intimidating Mr. Kelly tells us and

Ian nods. He drags me up to his room and closes the door a bit, leaving it barely cracked. I sit on his bed and scrub a hand down my face.

"I didn't know you had two dads." I state dumbly. Ian glances at me and tilts his head to the side in confusion.

"Oh, I would have sworn I told you. Maybe not. Well yeah, Owen has always been my dad's friend and a few years after my mom passed away they began to date. I mean, it was kind of weird to start referring to the man I always called uncle as dad but he's pretty awesome." Ian explains and I laugh.

"He's pretty intimidating." I state, laughing nervously as I remember how fricken' big that man is. He could break my neck with one hand, I swear.

"He's not intimidating, he's just kind of tall. He's not all bad honestly, he's like a big bunny. He just looks creepy, and sounds a bit creepy. But once you get to know him you'll love each other." He explains and I resist the urge to snort because I doubt I'll ever love that man. Jeez, just those harsh green eyes that seemed to want to obliterate me on the spot will haunt me for eternity.

"Sure," I mutter and Ian laughs, before coming over to sit next to me.

"Don't worry about it right now." Ian says before his arms wrap around my waist. I glance at him before kicking off my shoes, pulling him into my arms, and leaning back on his bed. He rests his head against my chest and I kiss the top of his head. I close my eyes and tighten my hold on him because although I know I'm going to hurt him, even though I know we won't last, I want to protect him, want to hold him, make him happy. Because I'm in love with him.

I love him.

Chapter Fourteen

~ ~So the votes have been tallied, needless to say Jevy is winning, which is a bit concerning... Just bare in mind I had all this planned out from the beginning, your guys' input helped but didn't actually sway how this was going to go down. So er, um, just don't kill me >.>~~

{Chapter Fourteen}

One of my favorite quotes by Gandhi, "nothing is impossible for pure love" seems sort of like a total lie. I'm sure he was a smart man but I think he may have been a tad wrong now that I'm older and actually am in love. Things are impossible, even for true love. Even now, as I lay with one of the loves of my life in my arms, I know my plan will be impossible. There's no way I could have what I want, not in a million years.

I know what I'm thinking will never happen, and I know what I have to do. What I don't want to do, but must. I give one last long look at Ian, savoring the feel of his body curled against mine, his even breaths fanning over my shirt, his incredibly soft brown curls. Even his slightly sweet scent that's a mixture of cologne, laundry soap, and something that's just unique to Ian Kelly.

I know I shouldn't but I love him, just as much as I love Jer. I shouldn't love them both, it's not right. But I can't help it. I do love them, both of them. And it kills me that I have to hurt Ian. But I know it has to be done. I kiss him lightly on his soft lips, savoring the familiar feel of his lips against mine.

"I love you, Baby." I whisper quietly after breaking from the chaste kiss, not wanting to wake him just yet. I close my eyes and savor this moment because I know it won't last much longer. I open my eyes to watch Ian while he sleeps peacefully, unaware that this will most likely be his last peaceful sleep for a quite a long time. His dark lashes cascade against his soft skin, his breath fanning against my shirt covered chest, his eyes twitching every now and then, and all I can think is how amazing he is; beautiful.

I lie there with Ian in my arms, and I realize something troubling: there is no way I can hurt him. And I can only hope he understands what I have to tell him. I hope he takes it well because I don't want to hurt him.

"I love you so much," I whisper, my heart beating painfully in my chest as I try to remain composed because I have to stay calm while I do this.

"Ian." I murmur, moving a stray strand of hair out of his face. He groans and opens his tired gray eyes to look at me.

"Hey, how long was I asleep? I didn't mean to to fall asleep but I didn't get much sleep last night." he mumbles apologetically and I smile a bit despite the fact that he shouldn't be apologizing, I should be apologizing to him.

"It's okay, I don't mind." I assure because I know he needs this, this little bit of sleep he can get before I do what I have to. He nods and yawns before he buries his head against my chest.

"I don't want to get up." He groans.

"I know." I reply. I run my fingers through his hair and he groans again.

"Don't do that, I'm going to fall back to sleep if you do." He whines, succeeding in receiving a smile from me.

"I won't mind if you do." I reply honestly. Because as cowardly as it is, I'd rather be with him like this a bit more before I have to tell him. Though instead of going back to sleep he merely shakes his head and opens his incredible gray eyes to look up at me once more.

"No, no. I have to stay awake." He says and smiles up at me. "I want to spend time with you, not use you as a pillow."

I smile and cup his cheek in my hand, running my thumb over his jaw. I can feel his rough stubble against my fingers and savor it, savor his soft skin and impossibly light gray eyes that nearly look white. I take it all in before I finally force myself to do this.

"Baby, I have to tell you something." I state, but I don't know how to say the rest when his gray eyes look at me expectantly, love potent in his eyes. I swallow hard and bite my lip roughly, feeling a lump form in my throat that prevents me from speaking. My face must have given something away because his eyes widen and he sits up a bit to look down at me.

"Whoa, what's wrong? You look like you're going to cry. Oh my God, you're not going to cry right? Oh my gosh, are you dying?" he demands with wide eyes, obviously trying to lighten the mood but I can't bring myself to laugh.

"I..." I silently curse myself for being unable to say what I have to. Ian tilts his head to the side in confusion, worry seeping into his eyes as we silently watch each other.

"Ian," I start, taking his hand in mine. "I love you." His eyes lighten but I continue, forcing the words out. "But I love someone else too, and I know it's not fair of me to ask this of you but I don't want to lose either of you. I want to keep you both."

I nearly sigh in relief when the last word is out of my mouth but I barely get time to take another breath, to let that sink in. Ian's face contorts first in agony, betrayal, and finally disgust so potent it makes me flinch without him even having to say anything. But God, when he does say something it hurts worse than that expression.

"What the hell is wrong with you?" he demands angrily, ripping his hand away from mine as he gets off his bed. He walks back until he runs into his desk, seeming to try to distance himself from me as much as possible.

"Ba--"

"No," he growls fiercely and I blink in surprise. I've never seen him get this mad, I can see it though, clear as day. He's furious, he's shaking so bad, it makes me want to go and hold him.

"Ian, please." I start in barely a whisper but he glares at me.

"I thought you were different, I thought you would be different than him but you both are the same." He snaps and my heart stops as I get off his bed.

"I'm nothing like him." I whisper, taking a step towards him but he beats me to it by coming right up to me, only to push me back roughly. I wince but take a step back to give him his distance.

"How could you possibly say that?! You just told me you love someone else. You just asked me if I would be in some disgusting relationship with you!" He screams, shaking with pure rage potent in his eyes.

"Ian," I start but he growls and slaps me hard, pushing me back towards the door with such force I fall against it.

"Shut up! Get out of my house!" He yells and pushes me again when I manage to regain my balance. I can't move though, I'm stunned. What happened to my bubbly, talkative Ian? What happened to the guy who didn't even like killing bugs?

"Ian." I whisper in pain, biting my lip hard enough to draw blood in order to fight off any embarrassing tears pressing to get out.

"Get. Out." He growls, the threat obvious in his eyes. I numbly nod, fumbling with his bedroom door handle before I turn to leave. I stumble down the stairs, trying to find my calm in case I run into one of Ian's dads.

When I get to the front door I can barely rejoice in the fact that I didn't get questioned by one of his dads. However when I leave the house, silently closing the door, I realize I didn't quite make it home free.

Mr. Kelly, or rather Owen, is leaning against my car with his arms crossed. I can't even muster up a groan, or irritation at the fact that I just had my car washed and I doubt his dirty looking leather jacket is clean. I don't comment though, a dirty car is honestly the least of my problems. I just numbly walk over to my car, taking my keys out of my pocket.

"What do you want? Want to rub salt in my wounds and tell me I need to watch my back because I hurt him?" I demand, suddenly very tired. He shrugs but sighs, dropping his arms to his side in a less threatening manner.

"No," I huff a weak laugh at that, shaking my head.

"No?" I repeat.

"You look pretty beat up as it is, and though you may not believe this but I'm not so sadistic that I'd kick you while you're down. It was quite obvious from the yelling that you hurt my son," he begins and I open my mouth to tell him I didn't want to but he cuts me a harsh glare that tells me to shut up and listen. "But it's also obvious you're pretty beaten up over the whole thing as it is, and me killing you for hurting my son won't really help any.

Besides, I know you love him, you just need to give him time." I shake my head, running a hand through my hair roughly.

"He's better off without me anyway, time won't help." I reply.

"If you believe that then maybe you really aren't fit to be with him." He grumbles and I glare at him but he returns it tenfold, leaving me to take an unconscious step back in self preservation. "Look kid, I haven't seen Ian so happy in a really long time. I haven't seen him sleep so peacefully since that bastard hurt him. You make him happy, and if you really love him you'll find a way to get him back. And if you can't get him back you don't deserve him. Now be safe, the roads are bound to be slippery, and it's about to rain." He adds before leaving me in confusion while he retreats back into the house.

I sigh though and unlock my car before getting in to head home. Of course it begins to rain like Owen predicted so I get rained on when I get to my house and get out of my car to go inside. I get in the house and take my jacket and boots off at the front door before I go to my room. I lock my door, strip my clothes, turn off the lights, and collapse in my bed. I hug a pillow tightly to my chest and close my eyes tightly, willing myself not to break down. But that doesn't work I realize when the hot trails begin down my cheeks, falling into my pillow.

I should have known he would react like that. Who wouldn't react like that? Who in their right mind would actually agree to what I had proposed? I should never have said anything, I should have just kept my mouth shut. But then what would I do about my feelings for Jer? I couldn't just stop talking to him, stop seeing him, and ignore what I feel. Because Jer is just as important to me as Ian.

I love them both, and I can't choose either of them.

I just, can't.

No, I won't. I'm not going to choose between the two. I refuse to do that because I love them both, I need them both in my life.

Chapter Fifteen

{ Chapter Fifteen}

"Leviathan Newark! Why are you still in bed? You're already going to be late for school as it is, you don't want to be any later." That's what I wake up to this morning, my mom yelling at me and shaking me violently as if that's going to urge me to get up.

I don't bother telling her that I'm skipping today because she's going to nag me for sure. Not to mention she'd ask a hundred questions about why I'm skipping, and I can't exactly tell her the truth.

So when she leaves my room and after I turn on my radio, playing probably one of the sappiest break up songs ever made- Apologize by OneRepublic. I realize I can't skip today. Today is of course the last day of the project so I have to slap on a fake smile, hand in everything, and give my presentation.

It makes me groan heavily but prompts me to get out of bed anyway. I reluctantly change into a fresh pair of clothes, fix my disheveled hair, and ignore the deep black bruises under my eyes from the lack of sleep I got last night.

This is probably the worst day that I have to give my presentation. Scratch that, this is the worst day to give my presentation.

I decide to go with my original plan of skipping school but instead I just skip first period so I can take a proper shower. I remove my clothes once more, tossing them in the hamper even though they're clearly not dirty, and get into the shower, not bothering to glance at the mirror because I'm sure I look like a mess.

The steaming water cascades down my back and burns my skin along the way but it's a welcome distraction from my thoughts. Thoughts that have been stuck on Ian since last night when he kicked me out of his house and slapped me, or rather the other way around. Even now I can hear his harsh words, feel the sting of his hand slapping me. The feel of his surprisingly strong arms pushing me into his door.

Though those memories hurt ten times less than the memory of his body lying with me, sleeping peacefully. His gray eyes looking at me with love.

Because it's those memories, the good ones, that kept me up all night while I wished over and over that I didn't say anything to him.

I sigh heavily, cupping water in my hand to splash against my face. I finally get out of the now lukewarm shower, shutting off the water then wrapping a towel around my waist. I leave the bathroom and retrieve a pair of black jeans and a white t-shirt from my closet. I put the clothes on and slip on a pair of black boots before I grab my things to leave the house.

I slide into my car, plugging my phone in so I can continue listening to Apologize on a loop despite the fact that the song is so overplayed, not to mention it's not exactly my type of music. I don't mind though, because although I know every single lyric and can rehearse it by memory merely because of how much it's been played on the radio, it's the only song in my phone that won't make my mood worse.

I drive through the nearly deserted town, deserted because it's already half past eight and everyone is either in school or work. It's nice though since I don't have to wait so long for lights to change or cars to cross at stop signs. I get to the school in good time, which I guess is a good thing, though what isn't good is the fact that since I missed first period there aren't any good parking spots. So I'm forced to park in the back so far that it'll take a good ten minutes just to walk to the main school building and another five to grab my stuff then go to my next class before the bell rings.

When I finally get into the main building, apologizing quickly to the security guard's disapproving glare as I slip through the front doors right as the bell rings that signals first period is over. I make it to my locker before slumping against it and sighing heavily. I stay like that for a minute before finally turning and taking what I need for my next class out of it and trudging to said class.

The day seems to move at a snail's pace as I move from class to class, handing in homework and basically continuing in autopilot. Even my presentation, something that's worth a good part of the grade for my project, went by in a blur as I rehearsed what I had earlier written down for the speech and merely clicked buttons to change the slides on my PowerPoint.

No one seemed to notice though, they all clapped, the teacher nodded her approval, I guess it went well. Even at lunch while Jess and Lydia were bickering about the latest song they heard, or was it whether or not they'll move if Trump becomes president. I can't recall, but in any case they didn't seem to notice my disinterest in everything.

Though, when I was finally released from the hell that is school, and started driving to my mom's work, I realized something. I need to cheer up because not only am I sure Jer will notice my less than normal mood, I also know I'm probably being dramatic and stupid. I shouldn't be this upset about what happened with Ian, my happiness shouldn't rely on someone else.

But even if my rational mind knows that, my heart won't stop hurting from the loss.

Despite those thoughts I change the music on my phone to Rob Zombie so I'm not listening to sappy chick music and push all thoughts of Ian out of my head so I can focus on being happy. Yeah right, happy. I snort in indignation at that and turn up the song, making it thump through my speakers, to drown out my thoughts.

Halfway through Living Dead Girl I make it to my mom's work and park in my usual spot, realizing this is going to be the last time I'm here. The last time I'll step out on the cracked sidewalk that somehow always manages to trip me despite the fact that I know about the large divot in the cement, no doubt from something heavy falling on it. I'll no longer be whipping numerous dead leaves from the large oak trees off my windshield when I leave.

Even when I enter the office, I find myself realizing that I'll miss the snarky receptionist whose name I still can't for the life of me remember despite hearing the simple thing numerous times. I walk through the hall, passing my mom's office that's empty, and after making a mental note to ask Jer about that, I go to Jer's office. I knock on the door but there's no answer so I knock again, this time a bit harder. Still no answer.

I briefly wonder if Jer took my mom out to lunch, or took her on a meeting for lunch, but then I recall seeing his black 4Runner parked outside so he's obviously here. I knock once more on the door but when there's still no answer I try the handle. It's unlocked so I go ahead and push it open, blinking as my eyes adjust to the dark room. The only light in the room is coming from the open door, flooding the light from the hallway into some of the room.

I close the door behind me, not really thinking about the room being dark, and feel around for the light switch. I find it pretty quick and flick the lights on, blinking a few times so my eyes will adjust to the sudden change in light. Then I gasp when my eyes land on Jer, shaking in the corner with his arms wrapped around his legs and head resting on his knees.

I honestly don't know what to do at first, I never thought Jer could look so vulnerable, so young. I do however find myself locking the door and carefully making my way over to him, avoiding the papers strewn all over the floor, the fabrics and clothes and even Jer's cell phone. I bend down in front of him, noticing that his eyes are closed tight and he's mouthing some words I can't catch.

"Jer," I touch him and he jumps, before trying to push himself back further but he's already as far in the corner as he can get. His eyes open and he seems to relax a tiny bit when he realizes it's me in front of him.

"Levy," he chokes out, his bloodshot eyes glancing around the empty room in fear.

"What's wrong?" I ask, reaching out to place my hand on top of his that are now resting on his knees.

"I heard them, they were here, I swear I could hear them." He whispers. I tilt my head to the side in confusion, wondering who he's talking about.

"Who?"

"Them, my parents. They were yelling at me, I could hear it, I could hear my dad." He shudders and fear flashes through his eyes before he shuts them tightly and bites his lip. His hands clamp around his knees, digging his nails into them.

"Hey, hey, hey. Calm down, look at me." I order softly. His eyes open and I smile a bit. I gently pull his arms from his legs and pull them gently. He seems to understand because he moves into my arms and rests his head on top of mine. The position in general is actually pretty awkward, as he's half on his knees, kind of hugging me while I'm also on my knees. But I ignore that and keep my arms around him nonetheless to comfort him.

He doesn't say anything for a while but his body slowly begins to relax, the shivering ceasing. He seems to take a couple deep breaths but even when he seems to be calm he doesn't move. I let him stay like that for a few more minutes in case he's still trying to calm down but finally I break the silence.

"Jer," I start and he pulls away, clearing his throat a bit.

"I'm sorry you had to see that." He mumbles, standing up and offering me his hand. I take it and he helps me to my feet. He brushes his pants off as if there's dirt on them then runs his hand through his hair, averting his gold eyes from mine.

"What happened?" I ask and he sighs a bit.

"It was nothing, I just had a small anxiety attack. I'm sorry if I alarmed you." He adds.

"You didn't alarm me. What were you talking about when you mentioned hearing your parents yelling?" I question, remembering how he had shuddered when he mentioned his dad. It sends an unwanted string of questions through my mind but I quickly push them away so as not to think about the possibilities right now.

"Nothing, they just used to yell a lot." He mutters in dismissal and though I know he's not telling me the full story I leave it alone because I know he'll tell me when he's ready.

"I'm sorry to hear that." I reply, and I really am. I couldn't imagine going through that, hearing my parents yell. I know they have occasional fights but they never yell at each other, they usually resolve it in less than an hour. Just the thought of having to hear them yell in anger makes me sad, I would hate it if they did. He shakes his head though, making some of his hair drop into his face.

"It's fine, I don't have to deal with that anymore." He says and though he's right, I know it's anything but fine. He obviously has problems because of his parents' yelling and he doesn't look fine either. It obviously affects him on a deep level, as it would for any kid who's parents yell. I don't say anything more though because I know he wants to drop the subject, so I change it.

"This is the last day of the whole shadowing thing." I state, grabbing his wrist and pulling him over to the couch. He just shrugs and takes a seat next to me.

"I know, it's kind of nice." He says and I smile a bit until he casually tosses his arm over my shoulders, pulling me a tad closer to him. It's not that I'm uncomfortable with the position but for some reason that makes me think of Ian, and my lack of communication with him. My lack of contact with him.

My heart seems to clench and I bite my lip before turning a bit to rest my head on Jer's chest. I take comfort in his strong chest, the muscles I can feel just under his shirt, the sound of his steady heartbeat. I know though, while I lie there in the comfortable silence, that I have to tell Jer about Ian. It's only fair I tell them both, they need to know.

I only hope Jer reacts better than Ian did because if he leaves me too, I'll be beyond crushed.

~~Fun fact; I actually nearly forgot to post this today. Oops :P~~

Chapter Sixteen

{ Chapter Sixteen}

"Jer, I have to tell you something." I state and pull away from him so I can look into his eyes. His golden eyes glance down at me in curiosity.

"What's wrong?" he asks immediately. I sigh and avert my eyes, scooting back a bit on the black couch to distance myself from him in case this doesn't end well. In case Jer reacts like Ian did.

"I need you to promise you won't get mad." I whisper and his eyes widen a bit in shock.

"Why would I get mad?" he questions, reaching out to take my hand in his. I bite my lip nervously and shake my head.

"Just promise." I reply softly. He watches me for a few minutes, his eyes showing his confusion and worry but eventually nods.

"I promise I won't get mad." He assures and I nod. I open my mouth to tell him but my heart begins to race, my palms sweating and a lump forms in my throat.

"I-I." I can't seem to get the words out, I'm so scared he's going to get mad, of course he's going to get mad. Who wouldn't be mad? Hurt, horrified. Disgusted. Just like Ian was.

"Levy, you can tell me anything, you know that." He soothes, running his thumb in circles over the top of my hand. The simple gesture seems to help some because my heart slows a bit and the lump in my throat eases.

"I love you," I state and something passes through his eyes but it's too fast for me to catch. I can however tell that he wants to argue that and I open my mouth to assure him I know what I'm feeling but he speaks before I can.

"How do you know?" he asks, surprising me because I honestly thought he'd argue, tell me I don't know what I'm feeling.

"Because I just know." I reply. I honestly don't know how to even begin to explain how I know I love him, because I can hardly understand it myself. All I know is whenever I'm with him, I'm happy, even when we're not talking--hell, even when I merely think about him--I feel better. He makes me happy, his presence makes me happy. I may not know him completely, and I know I'm young, but I know what love feels like. I know I love him.

"Okay," he says and I stare at him in surprise.

"Okay?" I echo. He shrugs and a smile slips on his face, making me relax a bit.

"I'm glad you feel that way, as long as you're sure about what you feel." He adds and I nod because I am sure. I know I love him, and even though it hurts I love Ian too. God, how did my life get this messed up?

I shake those thoughts away though and instead focus on what I was supposed to be telling Jer. I mean, I had to tell him that I love him but that's not what I wanted to tell him in the first place.

"There's something else." I mutter and he tilts his head to the side in confusion. Something passes through his eyes again but once more it's too fast for me to catch, however I swear it was something like, panic.

"What else?" he asks. I sigh and bite my lip again as I think of the best way to tell him. The best way to tell him so he won't get mad at me, if that's even possible.

"I am--well was--in a relationship. His name was Ian but that doesn't really matter. What matters is I love him too, and I know it's not fair of you to ask this but I can't choose who to stay with. I mean, I doubt it actually even matters now though because he's mad at me for telling him about my feelings for you and he broke up with me and only a crazy person would want to have this kind of relationship. Right?" I muse with a small but humorless laugh. Jer stares at me for the longest time, his eyes seeming guarded. I begin to panic because I can't tell if he's mad, surprised, hurt.

"You love him." He states and I nod. He laughs a bit and glances down at his lap before shaking his head and sighing.

"Wow," he sighs with another laugh. All the while I watch him, looking for any indication of his feelings, looking for any signs of anger.

"Are you mad?" I ask but he doesn't answer me.

"You want to be in a relationship, with both of us." He states and I'm not sure if it's a question or not so I answer regardless.

"Yes." I admit while I ignore my racing heartbeat. Is he mad? Is he disgusted that I would ask such a thing? Is he going to tell me he doesn't want that? Is he going to tell me I need to leave him alone?

The questions pester me to no ends and I want to ask him all those questions but I stay silent. Maybe if I stay quiet, he can have time to think about what I'm saying and hopefully won't react like Ian did. I mean, I probably told Ian at a bad time. He had just woken up, and I did drop the L word on him. Maybe he was just really surprised. And maybe I did it at the right time this time. Hopefully.

"Jer, please say something, you're scaring me." I finally mumble, scooting back a bit more on the couch and taking my hand from his. He blinks and looks first at his now empty hand before his eyes lock with mine. I can't read any of the emotions in his golden eyes, but I can only hope he's not mad. I can't handle losing both him and Ian. And so close together in time. I barely have had time to reel from the loss of Ian, I can't handle losing Jer right now.

Maybe I should have stayed quiet, told him later. Like on our date thing planned for tomorrow. That might have been a good time but he deserves to know before getting invested in this relationship.

"Okay," he says and I stare at him as confusion rushes through me.

"Okay? Okay what?" I demand, a tad hysterical.

"I'm okay with that, Levy." He adds. I can't help it, I just stare at him because I'm so surprised that he would say that. Who in their right mind agrees to that?

"Really?" I demand and he smiles reassuringly, reaching out to take my hand. He squeezes it gently and pulls me back to him by my hand to kiss me lightly on the lips.

"Yes. I feel something for you, stronger than any crush and if that's what you want I'll stand by your choice no matter what." He replies with honesty in his eyes and I feel my heart speed at that. I never thought in a million years I would meet anyone who's okay with what I want. I thought he was going to react like Ian did, yell at me for suggesting that. It makes me happier than I can begin to describe knowing he's okay with it.

"Thank you," I whisper and he smiles.

"You don't have to thank me, Love." He replies. I find myself smiling at that and he leans over to kiss me lightly once more before speaking again. "So what happened with the other guy?" he asks and I sigh.

I don't know if I should tell him, or rather I don't know if I'm ready to tell anyone. I can barely think about Ian right now without wanting to just, cry. I'm sure talking about him, telling someone about what happened will just be ten times worse than when I think about him, it'll make it more real, more permanent. Whereas if I kept it to myself, I can keep the foolish hope that I'll be able to talk to him and have him agree to my idea.

Then again, Jer deserves to know. Even if I don't want to talk about it, he's being so great as it is, he should know the full story. So I start from the beginning, admitting that I only started dating Ian because I wanted to get over Jer. I tell him about the moments we shared, when we would just lie there together in silence or when I would let Ian sleep since he never gets sleep without medication. I tell him about the first time Ian let me read his stories, and how nervous he was because his ex always put his writing down then wouldn't give him time to write.

And I tell him about Owen Kelly, Ian's scary dad. Then I explain the events of last night, trying to stay calm even with the lump forming in my throat. The memory begins to play on repeat in my mind, and it doesn't help that it's mixed with all the happy memories I had with Ian. It feels like a part of myself is gone, I feel half empty.

After I'm done I assume Jer's going to apologize or something, like most people do. But instead he just pulls me into a tight hug and kisses me lightly on the forehead. I rest my head on his chest and relish in the comfort of his arms, happy that they're helping me not think about Ian.

"Hey, I have a surprise for tomorrow." He says and though I can see he's obviously changing the subject, I appreciate it. He didn't just say he's sorry and try to make me feel better about Ian, and I'm glad he didn't because nothing he could say will make me feel better about that.

"What is it?" I ask, playing along with his subject change.

"If I told you, it wouldn't be a surprise now would it?" he muses and I laugh, shaking my head.

"Alright, I guess I can wait." I sigh dramatically and he chuckles before he leans down to kiss me lightly on the lips. I smile up at him and he smiles down at me, and everything seems right. In this moment there isn't any problems; there's no heartbroken Ian, no mom who I have to worry about finding out I'm not straight. It's just us alone, enjoying the moment.

Until it's shattered into a million pieces by a knock on the door.

I jump in surprise and scoot as far away from Jer as possible, leaving his comforting embrace in the process. Because I know that's my mom, the receptionist never comes to Jer's office, she just calls him. I think Jer realizes this too because he clears his throat, stands then wipes his shirt to smooth out any wrinkles before walking over to the door.

He unlocks it, as it was still locked it earlier when Jer was having a panic attack. He opens the door to reveal my mom, as expected, though what wasn't expected was her barging in and giving me a death glare. I flinch a bit, wondering why she could possibly be mad. Does she know about me? Me and Ian? Or worse, me and Jer?

"Mom," I say cautiously just as Jer says, "Sheryl, what's wrong?"

"Levy, I need to talk to you when we get home, so come straight home after this." Mom orders, looking like she wants to say more but her eyes glance at Jer and she seems to think better of it. Instead she walks out, leaving me in utter confusion. Why does she seem so mad?

Chapter Seventeen

{ Chapter Seventeen}

When I get home Mom is waiting for me on the couch in the living room with Dad, much to my surprise and worry. If both my parents want to talk to me I get the feeling it isn't going to end well.

"Hey," I greet them brightly despite having a bad feeling in the pit of my stomach about this. I put my backpack down by the couch and walk over to one of the two armchairs in the room to take a seat. After a moment of silence, with them looking at me while I stare at a small hole starting in my black jeans in interest, I clear my throat. "So what are we, uh, doing in here?" I question, keeping my voice bright.

"Your father and I have to ask you something, and I need you to tell the truth." Mom explains and I stiffen in my seat though I try to continue to keep my calm façade up.

"Oh?" I ask, my voice breaking a bit as the possibilities of what they could possibly ask me fill my mind. Does she know I'm gay? Does she know I'm attempting to start a relationship with her boss? Does she know about Ian? About the relationship I want with Ian and Jer?

"Levy, we know you've been hiding something from us." Mom starts and I swallow hard as my palms begin to get sticky with sweat. Is she going to demand I stop seeing Jer? Is she going to disown me for being gay? Would she really care?

My heart begins to beat rapidly and I feel a bead of sweat roll down my neck. I wait for what feels like an eternity for her to continue while I attempt to look calm, like I have nothing to hide. But her silence makes things worse as my heart pounds in my ear and drowns out whatever she finally does say. I blink, barely registering that her pink tinted lips are moving.

"W-what?" I stutter, realizing that my body is beginning to tremble with the panic. Mom looks irritated that I said that, no doubt assuming I wasn't listening to her.

"Are you doing drugs? You know, hopped up on mothballs." I stare at her in confusion.

"Mothballs?" I mutter in amusement, my heart slowing.

"I don't know what you kids call it now of days, Levy. I have to know if you're doing drugs. We can get you help if you are, we can tell everyone you have mono while you're in rehab." She adds with sincerity shining brightly in her eyes. I notice Dad is trying to stifle his snickers, covering them with coughs but Mom barely gives him a glance.

"You think I'm doing drugs? Wait, is that why you were glaring at me earlier today when you came into Jer, uh, Jeremiah's office?" I ask, quickly correcting myself because I know she'll harp on me for being so informal if I call Jer, Jer.

"Yes, of course. Why else would I be?" she asks, puzzled.

"Mom, I'm not doing drugs." I assure. "Why would you think I'm doing drugs? You know I've never been interested in all that party stuff." I add.

"Then what are you hiding?" she demands and I sigh in defeat. She's going to find out eventually, I might as well be the one to tell her rather than her finding out from someone else.

"I'm gay." I reply, biting my lip as my previous nervousness comes back full force. Mom stares at me for a few minutes and I notice Dad is looking at Mom, probably trying to gauge her reaction.

"You're gay," she states and I nod even though it was just a statement. "That's all?"

"That's all?" I echo half in surprise, half in disbelief that she actually asked me if that was it; as if the admission was trivial or something. "I thought you would be mad." I admit and she stares at me with an expression I can't interpret.

"Oh, Levy, I don't care. As long as you aren't doing drugs." She adds. I stare at her in disbelief.

"I'm not doing drugs." I manage to assure her, while I continue my attempt to calm down from the earlier panic. She nods her approval at that before shrugging.

"Well that's all. How did you do with your project?" she questions.

"I don't know, the teacher is going to give us a grade later." I mumble before clearing my throat. "Can I go?" she looks surprised at the question but nods with a smile.

"Well yes of course," she says with a chuckle and I nod, feeling numb. Of course when I stand both my parents stand with me and each hug me, probably showing their acceptance, or something. I honestly don't know what's going on in their minds but maybe they just wanted a hug, it doesn't really matter to me right now though.

I leave the living room and walk up the stairs to my room and push the off-white door open before walking across the room to fall onto my bed. I stay like that with my face against my comforter that smells like lavender. I realize my mom probably came in and washed my bedding, she always insists on doing the laundry when she's worried about something, even though I can—and do—do all my laundry myself.

I remember in fact one time when she washed my laundry and found one of Lydia's porn magazines that she insisted she keep at my house since her parents search her room all the time. I was barely thirteen and came home from school to have Mom ask me about it. Then she gave me the sex talk despite the fact that Dad had that talk with me a year earlier, and the school made sure I knew all about the reproductive system before I was even ten.

I finally sigh and push myself off my bed, shaking those memories away. I sit down on my bed correctly and contemplate what I should do. My first thought is to call Ian to tell him my mom didn't freak out about me being gay. But then I remember what happened and pain courses through me sharply. I swallow hard and lick my lips before I decide to busy myself with my homework.

There's actually a lot more than I originally thought and thankfully it takes me a few hours to complete with an hour break to eat dinner. I finish the last homework packet for Chemistry before I yawn and glance at the clock to see it's already ten. I put my homework and books away before I strip my clothes and turn off the light. I get in bed and close my eyes, clearing my mind so I can fall asleep.

~ ~ ~

I pull up at the school building, parking my car in the front, thankfully, and shut off my music. I get out of my car and lock it before I begin trudging up to the school building. Of course, this being not just Friday but also the night of a big football game against one of the private schools across town, everyone is excited and even more annoying as usual.

I walk past a group of jocks who are pushing at each other for some reason, a group of cheerleaders talking about the fact that someone named Stacy obviously gained ten pounds in less than a month which apparently means she's pregnant. I also overhear a group talking about how they're going to pull some kind of prank on the school today. And even the group of uninterested goth kids are hyped up about the game. I mean, I understand it's a pretty big deal because we haven't won against that team in the past five years, but I still don't understand why everyone can't just be calm.

I shake my head at the thought because I should know by now that I'll never be able to understand it merely due to the fact that I don't care about sports. Or winning a game against some kids I don't even know to get a pointless trophy and a title.

I walk through the crowd, pushing past bodies, until I finally reach my locker where Lydia is waiting. I contemplate telling her about Ian, and Jer, and everything else but I stop because as soon as I'm in hearing range she begins talking about Victoria.

I nod along and smile with her because she's so happy. Even though her parents still don't want her to see Victoria, and even though they can't be completely open with the relationship because her parents can't know, she's still happy. And I can't bring her down with my problems regarding love.

"So can you believe it?" she asks and I glance at her in question, narrowly dodging a football thrown by one of the football players.

"Believe what?" I question for clarification, opening the door to our class-room for her.

"That third quarter is already over. We only have a month, two? Until we graduate." She explains and I shrug. To be honest I haven't thought about graduation much in the last month, I've been a bit preoccupied. Even now, I doubt I'll think too much about it, I have other things to think about.

"I guess, it feels kind of weird." I admit because it does. It feels surreal. I've been in school for more than half my life, since I was five I've had to deal with school, yet it's all ending in just a couple months. We'll be released into the world as-mostly-adults, free to do what we wish. And in even less time than that, I'll be eighteen.

"It really does feel weird. So have you thought about your birthday? What are you going to do to celebrate?" she asks in excitement and I shrug.

"I don't know, go to a strip club?" I offer with a chuckle, ignoring the weird look the Chem teacher sends me as we walk past him. Lydia laughs and rolls her eyes, taking out her notebook along with the latest homework packet.

"Really? Somehow I doubt Ian would be okay with that." She says with a small round of laughter but it cuts off when she realizes I went silent. The thought of Ian sends a new bolt of pain through me, making me bite my lip hard to keep from saying or doing something I'll regret.

"Ian wouldn't care, he broke up with me Wednesday." I state in a monot-one. Lydia looks horrified and opens her mouth to speak but the teacher cuts her off when he starts the class. I don't pay much attention to it though because my mind keeps traveling to Ian.

I ignore Lydia's pestering questions when class is over and continue to ignore her when we part for our next class. It's not that I'm mad at her, after all she didn't make Ian break up with me, she didn't make me tell him I love Jer, and she didn't give me these feelings for Jer and Ian. She hasn't done anything to me, but I don't want to talk to anyone right now. I want to wallow in misery for the time being.

Of course I can't ignore Lydia forever and at lunch I don't have any reason not to tell her the full story. So I sit down at our lunch table after I get my lunch and reluctantly tell the girls what happened. As I tell the story, from start to finish about how Ian dumped me and Jer asked me out, they just "awed" or cooed at me. And when I'm finished, glancing down at my half eaten food, they "aw" at me again.

Honestly I find it incredibly weird and a bit awkward. They're not exactly the most caring people, so them showing this much affection is just, weird.

"You poor thing," Jess coos, moving out her seat to sit next to me and hug me. I glance at her out of the corner of my eyes in confusion until Lydia does the same thing.

"You totally deserve more," Lydia says, sitting on my other side and hugging me. I find it really weird, especially since they really aren't that affectionate, or so I thought. I can't help but snicker though at some of the jealous looks I receive from other guys in the cafeteria who are sitting near us, watching as two girls rub up against me and kiss up on me to make me feel better. If I wasn't so disheartened by talking about Ian I would find the whole situation quite hilarious.

"I'll be fine, I'll get over it." I assure but I'm not sure that's completely true. Ian is so special to me, even now, I don't know if I'll get over him easily.

"No, you have to get him back." Lydia states firmly, pulling away to look across me at Jess who seems to nod and look at me.

"And we're going to help."

Chapter Eighteen

{ Chapter Eighteen}

During lunch the girls only continued to whisper and giggle every now again about some plan to get Ian back. Though I just ignored them because I highly doubt two giggling teenage girls are going to be able to get Ian to forgive me, I wouldn't forgive me. The rest of the day was weird, what with actually going to our regularly scheduled classes rather than our parent's work. We didn't actually miss anything because we still did all our homework for those classes and kept up but it was definitely weird.

It wasn't until I actually got home that it sunk in that school was actually over and I was free to my own devices for the weekend. Then I remember my date with Jer and anticipation runs through me. Also curiosity because he did say he has a surprise for me.

So I use the next hour to get ready. I put on a nice red dress shirt, black jeans, and my nice black Vans to complete the outfit. I gather my stuff and leave the house after telling my parents that I'm going out. I drive to my mom's work, because Jer agreed that would probably be the easiest option rather than meeting in some location and leaving one of our cars at the place.

I shut the engine off, realizing I'm parked in my usual spot which makes me laugh a bit because I really thought yesterday would be the last day I parked here. That would be, or so I had thought, the last time I came here. I do get the feeling though that even this won't be the last time I come to my mom's, er, Jer's work.

After a minute or two I get out of my car and head into the building. I notice the receptionist is gone already, as is Mom obviously. I walk through the quiet, empty building, my footsteps echoing a bit throughout the halls. I go past Mom's darkened office, causing the lights to come on from the movement.

I get to Jer's door and get the familiar sense of deja vu. It was a mere thirty-one days ago that I first came to this exact door, pretending I didn't have the hots for my mom's boss. Just thirty-one days since I had pushed those feelings down, trying to ignore them. And barely less than thirty-one days that I met Ian. Barely less than thirty-one days did I somehow fall for both of them. And barely less than a week did I break one of the people I love.

Who knew so much could happen in such a small span of time.

"Levy, were you planning on staying outside my door all day? Or were you going to come in at some point?" Jer asks in amusement, his soft voice breaking me from my thoughts to look up at him. I laugh a bit and shake my head.

"Just thinking." I reply before leading the way out of the building. I notice Jer locks his office door before walking out and locking the front door of the building. He walks with me to my car but stops at the driver's door, making me look at him in confusion.

"Um, Jer I'm driving." I state and he chuckles.

"No, I have a surprise for you, so naturally I can't just tell you where to go. Now give me your keys," he orders in amusement and I sigh, begrudgingly handing him my keys. I get in the passenger's side, grumbling as I do while Jer just laughs and starts the car.

"You know, I've never actually driven a car this nice." He states before pulling out of the spot and putting my poor baby in drive only to peal out of the parking lot.

"Jeez, Jer, be careful with her." I grumble, grabbing onto the door handle as he takes a particular turn a bit faster than necessary.

"Don't worry, love, I won't hurt the car." He assures as he slows to a stop at a light. I relax into my seat at his assurance and sigh a bit.

"Yeah, ya better not. I love this car more than anything," I muse and he laughs, driving more like a sane person when the light turns green.

"I doubt that," he replies, reaching over to lock our fingers. I look down at our entwined fingers and smile, relaxing even more as he gets on the freeway. I watch as cars pass, watch the sights outside pass by as we go further out of town. Away from the lights, the drama, away from everything.

The car ride is quiet, save for the music playing softly through the speakers. Though it's comfortable, I don't feel the need to talk and I can tell Jer doesn't feel the need either. It's calming.

However, when we finally pass a sign declaring that we've come into the city next to our small town, I begin to become even more curious as to what Jer has planned. So I decide to break the calming silence, despite the fact that I know he's probably not going to tell me.

"So, where are we going?" I question, looking around at the bustling city. It's far bigger than our own town, much more populated with more stuff to do, large building and skyscrapers. It's not that our town is small, it's just more of a medium size. Not too large but not small in the least. So it does have things to do, and a couple thousand people. But it doesn't have an incredibly large range of things to do.

"Not gonna tell you, if I did it wouldn't be a very good surprise." Jer replies with a smirk and I sigh but I nod anyway. I decide to stay quiet, but my brain apparently has other plans because I don't stay silent.

"Are we going somewhere really nice?" I ask but since Jer doesn't seem to be dressed in formal clothes, rather he's wearing a plain white v-neck, and a leather jacket with gray jeans, I assume we're not going to a classy restaurant.

"Nothing fancy," he assures before taking an exit onto a road pegged Chester. He drives down the road a bit, making a few turns until he finally parks in a parking lot full of other cars. I glance around to see if I could find a sign for the restaurant but I don't see any so instead I just get out of the car. I meet Jer at the back of the car and he takes my hand before clicking my car's remote to lock it.

We walk into the restaurant, that isn't fancy like Jer had previously assured me of. It's just a small chain store with warm orange walls, multiple paintings, and a measly four couples. The place reminds me of a smaller, homier version of a Denny's. The smell of food is also quite potent, meats mixed with bastes and garlic, with a hint of fresh fish.

Jer leads me to the podium where a hostess is waiting. She glances up at our appearance and smiles brightly.

"Hello there, how can I help you?" she greets brightly, her bright blue eyes shining brightly.

"I have a reservation for two, under Cole." Jer responds and her blue eyes skim the list before nodding, making her blonde curls bounce a bit.

"Of course, you're seated right over here." She takes two menus and leads us through the less than crowded restaurant to an empty table for two. She sets the menus down in front of us while we each take our seats and after taking our drink order, leaves us alone.

It's silent for a minute while we look over our menus. While I'm scanning the dishes, I can't help but thank God for Jer bringing me to a restaurant where the menu isn't in some different language like I've seen happen in movies. That would be so awkward, trying to order something I can't even pronounce. I shake those thoughts away though and instead decide on some kind of steak that sounds good.

I fold my menu after deciding and Jer does the same just as the waitress arrives with our drinks. We both order and she assures us our food will be here soon before walking away with our menus. I take a sip of my water, watching Jer as he looks at his hand, twisting one of his rings around his fingers.

"What are you going to do about Ian?" he finally asks, looking up to meet my eyes with his gold ones. I swallow hard at that, biting my lip as I think about Ian. I haven't talked to him since he got mad at me, not that I've tried to talk to him. It's not that I don't want to talk to him, to try to get him back, but I'm honestly just scared that he's going to yell at me again. And I know that makes me a coward, but I can't help it.

"I don't know," I admit at last, dropping my eyes. I feel Jer's hand cover mine, giving it a squeeze in comfort, and I honestly nearly lose it. How did I find someone like Jer? Someone so accepting, accepting of the fact that I love not just him but someone else? How can he still stand me, let alone like me?

"Don't worry about it, Love. We'll figure it out." He assures and my gaze meets his once more as he smiles a bit. I honestly didn't think it was possible, but just his words, his smile, makes my heart flutter a bit with that familiar sensation of love.

"Thank you," I whisper, biting my lip a bit.

"You don't have to thank me," he replies honestly. I don't argue and we go quiet once more, but it's comfortable. The food comes soon after and we begin to eat. Surprisingly, Jer is the one to break the silence again.

"We're going to have to tell your parents, it's best they find out from you, or us, rather than let them hear it from someone else." He explains and I arc a brow in slight confusion.

"Tell them what exactly?" I prompt.

"About us; you, me, Ian." He clarifies softly. I stare at my plate for a minute or two, chewing my lip as I contemplate this.

"There is no you, me, and Ian if I can't get him to talk to me. Why tell my parents that there is a chance of us being in a relationship when right now there's no chance of that?" I question. Jer tilts his head to the side for a moment before shrugging.

"Because there will be an us. And we're going to have to tell them at some point. Honestly, Love, you overthink everything. But we can drop this for now." He adds before reaching over to wipe what I assume is a bit of steak sauce of my face and smirking as he licks his finger. Something about that movement makes me squirm in my seat a bit but I ignore it and continue eating.

The silence is, once more comfortable as we finish our meal. We don't get dessert and Jer pays. I don't bother arguing about that though because I know he wants to pay and will win the argument anyway. We get back in my car after leaving the restaurant and begin driving somewhere else.

I place my hand on top of Jer's on the gearshift and he glances at me a moment to smile a bit. The car is silent as we drive while I look out the window for any indication of where we're going. I watch bar after bar, store and even a strip club, pass by before Jer parks in the back of one building. I don't know where we are, and don't bother trying to find out because I know it won't actually help.

We get out and Jer leads me around front of the brown brick building. We enter the building and I'm confused at first until I realize where we are. An ice rink. I look over at him with a smile.

"Ice skating?" I ask in disbelief. He shrugs with a triumphant smile and leads me to the check in desk.

"Surprise." He says and I grin, stopping him from going any further so I can kiss him chastely on the lips.

"Thank you," I murmur against his lips. After that we get our skates and go over to the rink full of people, mostly couples.

I watch as people skate past us while we put on our skates, and all I can do is panic. These people are doing triple axles, lunges, and I swear one of them did some kind of back flip. And I'll be lucky if I can even stand on the skates.

"Jer," I whisper in worry, making him look away from his laces to me in surprise.

"Yeah?"

"I don't know how to skate. I can't even skate on roller skates." I inform him in a whisper as if the other people will hear and make fun of me.

"Oh, Love, don't worry about it. I'll be by your side through the whole thing." Jer assures with a small laugh before he finishes tying his skates. He helps me when he realizes I'm having a bit of trouble and finally stands, helping me stand as well. We walk over to the ice, which was actually easier than I thought it would be. It's actually not too hard to walk in these, I'm sure I'll be okay.

Or so I thought.

As soon as I'm on the ice I feel my balance shift and my legs shake as they threaten to give out. I ignore that and attempt to walk but yelp loudly when I realize I can't do it and begin falling back. Thankfully a pair of arms catch me before I could fall on my butt, and all I can do is sigh in relief.

"Dang, you really picked the worst person to skate with." I mutter as I struggle to turn in Jer's arms. He chuckles and leans down to kiss my forehead.

"You're doing fine. Just follow my lead and don't let go." He adds and before I can ask what he means, he's skating with me in tow by holding my hand. I gasp and clutch his hand in mine, probably hurting it but I can't think of that as we begin to glide across the ice. I realize after a few minutes that we're actually doing pretty good and I smile.

After a bit I get used to the feel of the skates and get a better handle on skating. Though I never let go of Jer's hand. Not that I would want to, just holding onto him sends bolts of electricity running through me.

It may not have been some kind of fancy date, with a pricey restaurant and some expensive play or something at the end. We didn't go on some balloon ride or anything like that. It was simple, yet thoughtful. It was perfect.

Chapter Nineteen

{Chapter Nineteen}

"Levy,"

I moan and open my eyes, cringing at the pain in my neck. I look around, noticing I'm in my car still, and realize I must have fallen asleep at some point after we got into the car from the ice rink. I glance outside my window to see where we are, and after blinking with a yawn I register that we're still on the highway back to town.

"Oh, sorry, I didn't mean to fall asleep." I say with a small laugh. I stretch as best as I can while in the car to try to wake up but honestly I still feel like if I close my eyes I'll fall asleep again.

"It's okay, love. I don't mind." I just nod, blinking slowly before my eyes shut again. I jolt awake though when my head falls forward and I blink rapidly in surprise.

"Oh crap, I did it again. I'm sorry, Jer." I mumble but he just laughs.

"It's alright, love, you didn't actually fall asleep though. You just closed your eyes a minute ago." He explains and I groan but nod.

"Right, right." I mutter, rubbing at my eyes. I realize though as we come closer to town, that I can't drive home, I'll fall asleep and crash. So either Jer is going to have to drive me home in my car and walk back to his office where his SUV is, or I'll have to leave my car at his office tonight so he can use his to drive me home along with himself.

I don't actually like either of those options. I don't want to leave my car out in the open like that, I mean this isn't a crime ridden place but there is a bad part of town, and hoodlums that think it's fun to ruin other people's stuff. And there is no way I can let Jer walk alone in the dark at, whatever time it is.

I glance at the clock, my eyes widening when I realize it's already past midnight. My eyes flicker from the glowing green numbers to Jer as I begin to worry about how we're both going to get home. I open my mouth to ask him just that but he interrupts me before I can speak.

"Levy, I don't think you should be driving. And I can't take you home, my office is too far away to walk from your house. Are your parents expecting you home tonight?" he asks, looking over his shoulder quickly before changing lanes to pass a slow moving blue Honda.

"Uh, no, it's Friday and I usually stay the night with Lydia on the weekends." I explain. Ever since we were little Lydia and I had stayed with each other on the weekends. Of course her parents weren't okay with it, only allowing it because of how much we begged and even then they made me sleep in the living room. That is until she came out to them and they assumed us staying together may lead to something that could apparently "fix" her.

So now they're always asking if I'm coming over because they still have it in their minds that we're going to do something, which is really disturbing. But nice because now the two of us can hide in her room with the door locked, blast music and do whatever we want.

In fact it was because of this that the two of us manged to get drunk our first time last year. But mostly we just watch TV and talk. Jer nods and I glance at him, waving my thoughts away to focus on his words.

"You could stay the night with me. We can take your car, leave mine at my office and you can just drop me off tomorrow to pick it up." He suggests and I stare at his silhouette for a bit in surprise. It isn't until a streetlight passes over us that I realize his expression is nervous, as if he expects me to reject his offer.

No, that's not it, I realize, he's not nervous about me rejecting his offer, he's nervous about me coming to his house. I blink in surprise at that realization that just brings more questions but I quickly push the questions away for another day so I can answer him.

"That sounds great," I assure before he can backtrack, because I can tell he was about to. He nods and I smile, reaching over to lace our fingers together on the gearshift.

The rest of the drive is silent, though probably mostly due to the fact that I keep dozing off, only waking up when my head falls foreword or we hit a bump. I can't help but rejoice when we make it into town and park in front of a nicely sized modern gray one story house. Jer shuts the car off and gets out while I yawn and send Mom a quick text to check in, telling her I'm with Lydia. At the same time I make sure to send Lydia a text to tell her to cover for me.

When I'm done I reach out to open my door but it opens for me and I realize Jer opened it for me. I smile at that, rolling my eyes as I stand but I nearly collapse as my legs were apparently nod ready to stand. Jer catches me though, laughing a bit against my neck. I huff but smile anyway, shaking each leg to make sure they're ready to be stood on.

"You okay?" Jer asks, reluctantly removing his warm, ink covered arms from around my waist. I nod, biting my lip a bit as I take a step forward. My legs seem to be okay, just a bit shaky, though I cling to Jer's arm anyway because I'm not sure I trust them not to give out again. Jer shuts my door softly before clicking it locked with the remote, shoving the keys in his pocket and moving towards his front door with me still hanging on his arm.

He doesn't seem to care though that I'm using him to level myself. He leads me up the three steps to his white door and digs around in his pocket for a minute before producing a set of keys. He unlocks his door, and if I hadn't been hanging on him, I wouldn't realize he's beginning to shake.

I want to ask him about it but I stay silent because I get the feeling he won't want to talk about it. So I keep my question to myself, pretending I don't know he's shaking while he pretends not to be shaking. It really makes me sad, because it's apparent something is wrong, and I get the feeling it has to do with his parents and his panic attack yesterday.

His parents had to have done something worse than merely just yell around or at him, and it honestly breaks my heart. But I push those thoughts away quickly, glancing around the clean, but kind of barren living room. He leads me through the room, filled with nothing more than a TV, desk, couch, chair and coffee table.

Through a doorway is a hallway, leading past a kitchen, dining room, a backdoor that probably leads out to a yard, and two doors on the right that are closed. Jer opens the one closest to us, revealing a nicely sized bedroom. Though, it's pretty empty too. Only a bed, desk, dresser, closet and a few other random things are in the room.

I also note it has two doors, probably one that leads to a bathroom and another leading to the room next to this one. I briefly wonder if the other room is a spare bedroom but I don't honestly care at this point because I'm exhausted.

"This is nice," I mumble past a yawn, covering my mouth in an attempt to stifle my yawn but it doesn't help. Jer nods with a small smile before leading me over to the bed, letting me sit down. It isn't very big, I honestly expected him to have a huge house with a huge bed, but the bed is just a regular double bed with a simple black quilt and white sheets.

"You should go ahead get some sleep, if you want I may have some pajama bottoms that may fit you." He offers but I shake my head with another yawn, kicking my shoes off and scooting back on the bed. I pull the quilt down along with the top sheet and after I discard my shirt to the floor I slide under the blankets. I yawn, closing my eyes until I hear Jer's footsteps retreating.

"Jer," I call, my voice terribly tiny as I attempt to stay awake a few more minutes despite my body trying to shut itself down for sleep in the comfortable bed. I force my eyes open to look at Jer in the dark, the only light coming from the streetlight outside his window.

The light is enough though because I can see the nervousness present in Jer's golden eyes, I can tell he's still shaking slightly and my heart clenches at that but I quickly banish those thoughts. I move my hand out of the comfort of the covers to outstretch to him, waving him over.

"Come here," I order softly. He looks reluctant but walks back to the bedside slowly.

"What do you need, Love?" he asks me, his voice barely a whisper. I smile though I'm not sure he can see it, and reach out to take his hand in mine.

"Get in bed, I'm tired and I want you with me." I add, thankful that it's too dark to see the blush on my cheeks from how embarrassing those words sound coming from me. He looks reluctant to oblige but nods slowly, removing his own shirt, jacket, and shoes before getting in the bed next to me.

At first he doesn't move and I can tell he isn't relaxing. But I move over to wrap one arm around one of his while I drape the other over his bare chest and rest my head against his chest. I kiss his chest lightly with a small smile while he begins to relax under me.

"Goodnight, hon'. I love you." I murmur, sighing in content as my mind begins to shut down for much needed sleep.

"Goodnight, love." Jer whispers in reply and I fall asleep as he begins running his fingers against my arm soothingly.

I wake way too early, the sun seeming to still be coming up, giving me just enough light from Jer's window to realize I'm alone in the room. The bathroom door is ajar and I can tell it's empty in there too so Jer has most definitely left the room. I groan, falling against the soft feather pillow behind me before I slide out of bed.

I shiver but make a mental note to thank Jer for having carpet rather than cold tile, laminate or wood flooring. I leave the room, looking around the hall and wondering where he went. I move to the living room until I catch sight of the back door that's open a bit. I contemplate going back in the room to put my Vans back on so I won't have to walk outside without them but I honestly don't want to so I don't worry about it.

I walk down the frigid hall, the cool air from outside seeping in from the open door and making goosebumps rise on my arms. I shiver but continue until I'm at the back door. I push it open, noticing there's a nice back deck so I won't have to worry about wearing shoes out. I walk out and see Jer leaning against the bright orange wooden railing of the deck with his back to me. I walk over to him and wrap my arms around his waist from behind him.

He stiffens but slowly relaxes when he realizes it's me. It makes me smile a bit as I rest my head against his back, closing my eyes. Until I smell the scent of cigarettes that I swear I've never smelled on Jer before. My nose scrunches up in distaste at the smell and I pull away to stand next to him, realizing he has a cigarette in his right hand.

"I didn't know you smoked." I state, staring at the glowing white cancerous stick between his fingers. He shrugs, lifting the cigarette to his mouth to take a long drag, exhaling the smoke slowly as he flicks the ash to the ground below us.

"I don't often, my parents hated this kind of stuff, so I kind of got used to not doing anything like drinking or smoking. But I like the flavor, and they relax me a bit." He explains with another unconcerned shrug. I watch him for another minute as my still-tired brain processes his words. There it is again, I realize, him mentioning his parents. That makes me wonder though, if his parents disproved of drinking and tobacco, what did they think of his tattoos? Piercings?

I continue to watch in silence while he stares out at the yard, enclosed by a large gray brick wall. He brings the cigarette up to his mouth once more, inhaling deeply before rubbing the butt out on the wooden railing and dropping the ruined thing onto the deck. He glances at me and smiles a bit, moving to wrap his arm around my waist.

"Come on, love, you look exhausted." He says as he leads me back in the house. It isn't until we're in the warm confines of the bedroom that I realize I'm freezing cold. I shiver and move closer into Jer's warm arms. He seems to laugh at this as he leads me back over to the bed, pulling the covers back so we can slide back in. I cuddle up against him, taking comfort in his body heat as I attempt to warm up.

He wraps his arms around me while I rest my head on his chest and close my eyes. After I warm up a bit more I find myself yawning as my previous exhaustion comes back, and soon I'm falling back to sleep. Happy for the moment in the arms of one of my loves.

Chapter Twenty

{ Chapter Twenty}

I wake to the sweet smells of breakfast; pancakes, maple syrup, powdered sugar, and the likes. I open my eyes after I register all the scents permeating the air, and blink a few times to focus my eyes. I first notice the off-white paint on the ceiling, and though confusion seems to run through me for a minute at the unfamiliar color, I remember I'm not in my own room, or rather not my own house.

I stretch and yawn after I remember what happened last night before I turn to see if Jer is still in bed. As I suspected, he's gone, probably in the kitchen where I assume the smells of breakfast are coming from.

So of course, I decide to go ahead and get out of bed, though when my feet hit the soft black carpet, I realize I have to pee. I stand, stretch again while a few of my joints pop, and head to the bathroom across the room. After I relieve my bladder and flush, washing my hands, I run a wet hand through my hair in an attempt to fix it. It doesn't do much to help but my hair doesn't actually look too bad in the first place so I don't bother with it anymore.

I leave the bedroom, vividly recalling where the entrance to the kitchen is despite my memory of last night being a bit fuzzy because of how tired I was. I walk through the familiar hall, walking through the doorway to the kitchen. I stop in the doorway though, watching in amusement as Jer sways his hips in time with the music playing softly through the speakers on the walls while he flips a pancake.

I contemplate interrupting him by calling out to him but instead I silently move across the cold gray laminate tiles of the kitchen until I'm behind Jer. I smile a bit before I place my hands on his hips then I snake them around his naked waist. He jumps in surprise, dropping the metal spatula onto the iron skillet, making a loud clanging noise resound in the kitchen.

He turns in my arms, relaxing slowly as an amused smile graces his lips. He lifts a hand to move a piece of hair out of my face before leaning down to kiss my forehead.

"How long have you been up?" he asks curiously.

"Not long," I say with a shrug. "I only woke up a few minutes ago." He nods in understanding before leaning down to kiss me on the forehead once more. Then he turns back around to flip the pancake onto the plate beside the stove that holds a stack of them. I drop my arms from Jer's waist so he can lead the way into the dinning room where a sleek black and white table is holding the rest of our breakfast. There's two spots set at the table despite there being six seats, with a bowl holding what must be eggs, a plate of bacon, and a pitcher of orange juice.

It's honestly what I would expect a normal family breakfast to look like, not that we don't have breakfast together but Mom and Dad tend not to be home early in the mornings, plus they sleep in on the weekends. Of course, we have dinner together when I'm home, but something about this seems different than a normal family breakfast would be. And when I glance over at Jer who's setting the plate of pancakes on the table, I can tell this is more personal for him.

That makes me smile a bit as I take a seat at the table. Jer leaves the room for a second only to come back with a black mug, probably holding coffee. He sits down across from me and we fill our plates with food before we begin to eat. Or rather I eat while Jer closes his eyes for a moment, confusing me until I realize he's probably praying. My parents pray before their meals also, though apparently the habit didn't rub off on me.

"What are you going to do about Ian?" Jer questions while sipping on his coffee after his eyes open once more. I sigh, resisting the urge to drop my head on the table, mainly because I'm enjoying this food.

"I don't know," I reply honestly, casting my eyes down to my food while I try not to think of Ian. I finish my eggs before I run a hand through my hair, glancing up to look at Jer who seems to be watching me intently.

"I need to talk to him, don't I?" I ask before rolling my eyes, taking a bite of my pancake and swallowing before I huff. "Of course I need to talk to him, but what if he doesn't want to talk to me? What if he tells me to go away? What if he doesn't listen to me? What if he hates me?" I groan.

"Ugh, I just need to talk to him don't I? I need to man up." I grumble then look back at Jer who has an amused expression on his face. "Any advice?"

"Be careful, love. If he doesn't want to talk to you, don't force him. He'll come around eventually, you just need to be patient. But if he lets you talk don't hold back." He adds seriously before finishing the rest of his food. I glance down at my own plate, realizing I only have one piece of bacon and a few bites of my syrup covered pancake left on the square black plate.

"Will you help me?" I ask, pushing my plate away after eating the last bites.

"I'll help you with the plan, but I doubt talking to him with you would do much good at this time." He replies and I nod.

We're silent for a few minutes before we begin clearing the table and putting the leftovers away in the fridge. When everything is cleaned up Jer leads us to the living room where he pulls me down with him on the couch. I fall beside him and he wraps his arms around my waist from the side, dropping his head to my shoulder.

"You need to be attentive when talking to him, be careful with what you say. And don't get mad at him." Jer adds sternly, moving a bit to stare into my eyes seriously. I attempt not to laugh but I fail miserably as I begin to snicker before I drop my head on his bare shoulder. I shake with the laughter, trying to contain it but I barely do as I regain my composure.

"What?" he demands and I pull back to look up at him.

"Jer, you're making him seem like a girl who's going to break down at any second." I explain, laughing a bit more because of how serious he was. "Look, I get that Ian is hurt, and rightly so, but he's not going to shatter if I'm not attentive. He's stronger than that." I add, my mind wondering to Ian. His beautiful nearly-white gray eyes, his adorable ramblings and the way he felt in my arms. It felt right to hold him, to comfort him, to kiss him.

"Just be careful, love. I don't want you to get hurt." He replies, pulling me into his arms as he lies back on the couch. I sigh, moving so I'm hovering above him, taking in his beautiful body under mine. His unique golden eyes, his pink lips tipped in a small smile, even his light stubble he's failed to shave off today seems to look perfect on him.

"What are you looking at?" he asks with a knowing smirk, as if he knows how sexy he looks right now.

"You," I reply honestly, moving my hand to rest on his bare chest, covering a black tattoo of an arrow in an infinity symbol.

"Oh yeah?" he muses and I smirk, leaning down to kiss him. I run my hand along his chest and lick his bottom lip for entrance but he pushes me a bit. I pull back to look down at him in confusion and he sighs, lifting a hand to caress my cheek.

"Although I want to continue with this, I think it would be best we don't or else I won't be able to let you leave." Jer explains with a chuckle and I sigh, dropping my head on his chest.

"I get it." I reply honestly and move to get more comfortable. I close my eyes when I'm comfortably in his arms with my head resting comfortably against his chest, allowing me to hear his strong heartbeat. I sigh in content, contemplating the idea of just staying here all day. It is the weekend after all, I should be relaxing.

Of course, the longer I put off talking the Ian, the harder it's going to be. Or the less I'll want to do it. In any case I need to talk to him, not fall asleep on Jer, no matter how comfortable or comforting he is.

"Don't fall asleep, love." Jer calls but I ignore him, keeping my eyes closed as I listen to his relaxing heartbeat.

"But this is so relaxing," I finally mumble my response, moving slightly to kiss his chest.

"I know, but you have to talk to Ian. And I'm sure your parents are expecting an appearance from you at some point today." He reminds but that doesn't seem to stop him from running his fingers through my hair.

"That doesn't help motivate me, you know." He laughs, the sound vibrating through his chest and into my ear.

"I'm sure it doesn't." I expect him to continue running his fingers through my hair but he doesn't, instead he moves, making me move away from him as he sits up. He stands and wipes at his pajama bottoms before extending his hand out to me to help me up. I sigh, grumbling under my breath about how I didn't want to do anything today, but take his hand regardless.

I stand with him and follow him into the bedroom. He moves to his closet to get a change of clothes before moving over to me, kissing me lightly on the lips.

"I'm going to get dressed and you can drive me back to my car. Then you have to talk to Ian." He adds sternly before going to into the bathroom and closing the door behind him. I sigh, my eyes falling to the floor where my shirt that I barely remember taking off last night, and my shoes are lying. I stoop down to pick up my shirt, dropping it on Jer's bed before pulling my shoes on.

I grab my phone from the night stand and unlock it to check my messages. I notice I have two unread messages, one is a reply from Lydia about covering for me, while the other is from Mom asking if I'll be home today. I don't bother replying to either of them and instead stuff my phone in my pocket. Jer comes out of the bathroom just then wearing a white v-neck that actually seems a bit transparent as I can make out his tattoos through the shirt. He's also wearing a pair of black jeans with a pair of boots.

"That shirt is a bit revealing." I state, eyeing his attire once more, stopping to look at his right arm where a thick black cross starts at his forearm and ends a little bit above his wrist, nearly encircling his arm completely.

"Does it bother you?" he asks.

"Not at all," I reply, picking my shirt up off the bed, not bothering to put it back on because it's dirty and I'm going straight home anyway to change. I glance around before my eyes move back to Jer. "Where are my keys?" I question when I remember he was driving so he no doubt has them. He motions for me to follow him and I do, trailing behind him while he grabs his phone, wallet and keys off an end table in the living room before picking my keys off the table. He tosses them to me and I nod, following him out of the house.

He locks the door behind him and follows me to my car. I glance around as I move to my car, taking in the bright green grass, the flowers growing close to the sidewalk, and a hedge separating Jer's yard from his neighbors. I unlock my car, get in and wait for Jer to get in before I drive towards his office.

The drive is silent but Jer keeps his hand resting on my thigh the whole time, making me smile just a bit. Unfortunately the drive isn't too long so we get there in a little less than fifteen minutes. I park next to his 4Runner and turn to say goodbye when he pulls me in to kiss me chastely.

"I'll see you soon, love." He whispers, kissing me again and running his fingers through my hair before opening his door to get out.

"Jer," I blurt, biting my lip a bit when he turns, leaning back into my car. "I love you." I state and he smiles.

"I'll talk to you later, love." He replies before shutting the door and getting into his truck. I put my car in drive and leave his office, heading home. I park behind Dad's black truck and shut off my car. I walk over the yellowing grass to our front door, checking to see if it's unlocked which it is. I push the door open and walk into the warm house, hearing soft music playing in the living room.

I tilt my head a bit in confusion before moving silently to the living room so I can investigate the noise. I stop though, smiling fondly when I realize my parents are slow dancing. I lean against the door frame in the living room, watching as they dance across the room, spinning and twirling; laughing and smiling as if they were two teenagers in love. And they are in love, it's obvious from the look in both their eyes, they love each other so much.

I realize, as I watch Dad twirl Mom, dipping her before pulling her up to him to kiss her while she laughs joyously, I want that. In thirty years I want to be just as in love as they are, I want to dance with my husband for no reason and laugh with them. That's what I want, I want them-Ian and Jer-no matter how hard it'll be. Because I know without a doubt in my mind that I love them both to death and whatever I have to deal with to be with them will be worth it.

With that in mind I start up the stairs and plan how I'm going to talk to Ian today, what I'm going to say. Because I need to get him back, no matter how long or hard it'll be.

Chapter Twenty-One

{ Chapter Twenty-One}

After I get out of the shower I put on a pair of clean blue jeans, a dark blue shirt, and boots. I fix my blonde hair by running a quick hand through it before slipping my phone into my pocket. I pick my keys up off my bed and glance around, trying to think of something I may be forgetting. Maybe I forgot to do something, anything that could prolong the inevitable talk with Ian.

I want to talk to him, I really do, but at the same time I'm terrified that he's going to get mad at me again. Hell, I'm giving myself the benefit of the doubt, what if he doesn't even talk to me? Or God forbid his dads decide not to have pity for me and instead follow through with their threats to kill me for hurting Ian.

But I guess, as Mom says, I never know until I try. I can't possibly know if he'll talk to me or not unless I try to talk to him.

So with a small, very small, amount of resolve I manage to step out of my room. I close my door and heave a sigh as I make my way down the stairs. I pass by the living room, noticing Mom and Dad are watching some movie on the TV, no doubt enjoying their time with each other while they're both off work.

"I'm going to hang out with some friends, I'll be back later. If not I'll call." I add and Mom waves her hand to me without taking her eyes off of the animated movie.

"Okay, sweetie, we'll see you later. Tell me if you won't be back for dinner." She adds sternly and I smile a bit.

"Okay, Mom. See you later. Love you guys." I add before passing the living room and moving to the front door. I pull it open, close it behind me, and walk across the lawn to the car.

I unlock it with the remote and slide in, plugging my phone into the speakers to play music. I shift into reverse and pull out of my driveway, a pool of dread filling my stomach. I drive past houses in a blur, hardly registering the lyrics of the song playing in the car right now. Hardly registering anything actually.

I had no idea I could feel this nervous about talking to someone, but apparently I can. What if Ian doesn't want this? What if he tells me it's either him or nothing? I can't leave Jer, I can't. But I can't not be with Ian either, I love them so much.

I jump in surprise when a loud honk sounds from outside the car, making me realize I've been idling at this now-green light longer than I should. I quickly pull off the brake and turn into the small neighborhood where Ian lives. I pull up to his house minutes later, groaning when I see both Ian's dads' cars in the driveway along with Ian's car.

I put the car in park, take the keys from the engine and sit in the car for a few minutes. I look down at my black leather steering wheel, the gold Chevy emblem molded into the horn. Of course, I realize I'm only stalling by doing this so I force myself out of the safety of my car and force my legs to move across the yellowing grass of the lawn to the front door.

I put my hand up, swallowing hard before I knock three loud times on the door. A minute or so later none other than Owen Kelly in his leather clad, six foot something glory, answers the door, staring at me with some sort of emotion I can't decipher. I can only hope it isn't anger, fury, or anything remotely similar.

"Levy." He states in a monotone.

"Uhm, yeah, hi Mr. Kelly. I know you probably want to kill me but--"

"We were expecting you." He interrupts me and I stare at him in confused curiosity. Why would they be expecting him? Them as in who exactly?

"Oh?" I squeak, the possibility of getting murdered and made into dog food makes me more nervous by the minute. It doesn't actually help that I told Mom I was with friends, so no one knows I'm here. Except Jer. That eases a small amount of my nerves but it doesn't help too much.

However, when Owen opens the front door wide, stepping aside to let me in, I realize I probably don't have too much to be worried about. So I step through the door, hearing it close behind me once I'm inside the warm house.

"He's in his room, go on up but...be careful." Owen adds with a shrug before moving past me to some other part of the house, probably to torture the innocent or something. I roll my eyes at my own thoughts, moving through the familiar homey hall up the stairs and straight to Ian's bedroom door.

I stare at the piece of painted wood as if the Devil himself made it before I gather my courage and knock. After a few seconds without a response I decide to try the handle, realizing it's unlocked. I push the door open, slipping into the room quickly before closing the door behind me. I turn back and smile a bit when my eyes land on Ian's messy brown hair.

He's sitting with his back to me at his desk, typing so fast I'm surprised he isn't breaking the computer keys. Hell, I'm surprised he can even type that fast without his fingers hurting. Nonetheless I do realize he also has his earbuds in, mostly because I can hear the hints of heavy metal all the way over here. It bugs me that he's blaring music, especially heavy metal, as that could damage his hearing severely but I push those thoughts away. This is not the time nor the place to lecture him about the dangers of hearing loss.

I move across the room, resisting the urge to wrap him in my arms and tell him I'm horribly sorry. Instead I stop behind him, reaching out to touch him but I pause when my eyes land on the words he's typing so quickly.

"Do it Ares and everything will be okay, I promise." The devil coaxes in my ear. No one but me can save myself, but it's too late Now I can't think, think why I should even try Yesterday seems as though it never existed Death greets me warm, now I will just say goodbye Goodbye...

I force my eyes away from the screen and instead rest my hand on Ian's shoulder. He jumps but doesn't turn as he continues to type furiously.

"Leave me alone, Owen. I already ate today, I'm fine." He mumbles, his voice so low I can hardly hear it. It's so rough, so different from his usual bright, bubbly voice.

"Ian." I call, shaking him a bit.

"Owen," he growls in the same gravely voice that tells me he hasn't had anything to drink in a while. He yanks his earbuds out and turns in his swivel chair to glare at me but his face goes completely blank when he realizes it's me, not his scary dad Owen.

My heart, of course, breaks and soars at the same time. I love seeing his beautiful nearly white, gray eyes, his kissable lips. But at the same time I can tell something is off. His usually bright gray eyes are dark, his lips turned down in nothing resembling his usual carefree smile. He looks exactly the same but somehow completely different.

"What are you doing in my room?" he demands, shutting the screen on his laptop before standing from the chair.

"I want to talk to you," I reply honestly. He stares at me, unblinking before he runs a hand roughly through his brown hair, moving past me to his bed.

"No, you're not supposed to be here. I told my dads not to let you in." He states as he pulls his nightstand drawer open as if searching for something. He apparently doesn't find it because he heaves a deep sigh before closing the drawer roughly.

"Hear me out," I plead and he turns to me, eyes sharp.

"Why?"

"Because I can't stand not being around you. I lo--"

"No." He growls, taking a few threatening steps towards me but apparently thinks better of it because he moves to his bed, smoothing out a wrinkle in the blanket.

"Yes, I love you Ian. And I hate that I can't talk to you. I miss you." I add. He snorts, moving across the room to move a few books around on the large bookshelf he has.

"Jansen goes after Janknis." He mumbles and I stare at him for a minute in utter confusion. Who is Jansen and Jenknis? What does that have to do with us?

"What?" I ask in utter confusion and he turns to me, a foreign emotion in his wide gray eyes. It's a stark contrast to his previously blank face but whatever that is, it isn't something I ever want to see in Ian's eyes. It looks almost insane, or lost.

"How did I not see it? I put Marr in front of Mannuel." He states, turning back to the bookshelf and removing numerous books. I realize he's talking about the authors. He's putting them in alphabetical order. I still have no idea why he's worrying about that right now of all times and it bothers me quite a bit.

"Um yeah, R would go after N. Ian, are you listening to me?" I whisper but he merely mumbles things to himself.

"Black. Black eyes. They were horrible." He mutters, removing half the books on his bookshelf and putting them on the floor.

"Who had black eyes?" I question, moving towards him cautiously. I figured he wouldn't be too happy to see me, and would probably be mad, but I don't even know what's going on. He doesn't seem mad, he is talking to me so that's something. But he's definitely not his self, something's wrong.

"He did. He was so nice. So handsome. But his eyes, they always felt wrong." He continues, seeming to be talking to himself. Something is definitely wrong, and it's making me wonder if I should call out for one of his dads, maybe they know what's going on.

"How were they wrong?" I probe, relieved he's talking to me but increasingly worried about what's wrong.

"Evil." He replies, looking up at the ceiling, seeming to completely forget about the books.

"Evil?" I echo while he nods.

"His eyes were evil. I ignored it, I liked him. A demon in a pretty mask." He adds with dead laughter I would never expect to come from him. It's so empty, devoid of any emotion; it makes me flinch.

"Dads were gone, they had gone out for dinner. He came over, I knew something was wrong. Something felt wrong. It feels wrong." He states, seeming to relive some kind of memory.

"Something's wrong with him. I don't ask about it though because if I bring it up he's going to be mad. I don't want to make him mad again. He's leading me to the bedroom. Why is he leading me to my room? I thought we were watching movies."

My heart clenches as I realize, probably too late, what he's remembering, or reliving rather.

"Ian, look at me." I order but he doesn't seem to hear me as he mumbles a few things to himself. "Ian." I hiss, moving to stand in front of him but his eyes are closed as his body begins to tremble.

"He locks the door behind us, I don't know why though. My dads are gone so what's the point? When he turns to me his black eyes lock on me. It's uncomfortable. I don't like this look, it's different then most of the looks he gives me. I have to ask him what's wrong. But if I do he might get mad. I should just stay quiet like he's told me to do so many times before. I need to shut up like he says."

"Ian, open your eyes." I try again, waving my hand in front of his closed eyes.

"What are you looking at? I have to ask with a small laugh. He seems to lick his lips before moving towards me quickly. I don't realize what he's intending to do until his fingers are fumbling to unbutton my jeans. No. Stop. He doesn't. No, stop. I don't want to do this." His breathing becomes more labored and I begin to panic. I don't know what to do. I don't want him to go through this, not again.

"Ian, baby, look at me. Open your eyes, babe. Look at me, focus on me. On me, Levy, not him." I urge, reaching out to touch him but he flinches.

"No." He gasps in pain and my heart shatters.

"Baby, come on, look at me. Open your eyes, please." I add, reaching out one more time to touch him. He doesn't flinch this time so I quickly pull him into my arms, tightening them around him as I whisper soothing things in his ear while stroking his hair.

"Come on babe, stop thinking about that. Focus on me." I whisper and he gasps. He pulls away from me quickly, stumbling back as his eyes go wide when he looks around his room.

"Oh god." He mumbles, his eyes becoming glassy as he tries to hold back tears. My heart clenches and I bite my lip hard before I pull him into my arms.

"It's going to be okay, babe." I murmur softly as I run my fingers through his hair soothingly. "I promise."

Chapter Twenty-Two

{ Chapter Twenty-Two}

"Are you sure you're going to be okay?" I ask worriedly. Ian nods, his eyes closed while I continue to stroke his hair. I have to go talk to Lydia who called me a minute ago in near tears, mumbling something about being at the park and her parents. I obviously need to make sure everything is okay but I don't want to leave Ian after what happened a little over an hour ago.

"Go, I'll be okay." He assures in a tired voice and I nod slowly though he can't see it.

"I'll be back." I state, stooping down to kiss him on the forehead. He nods slightly so I grab my keys off the nightstand and leave his room, keeping his door open. I make my way through the house, passing the living room where Owen and Haiden are talking. They seem to stop when I pass but I wave it off until Haiden calls my name.

I bite my lip, reluctantly moving back to the living room. I enter and notice the two have a movie muted on the TV, not seeming to care about it.

"Uhm, hi." I mumble, averting my eyes from Haiden.

"Why don't you have a seat?" Haiden offers and when my eyes return to the two I realize they don't actually look angry. Then again, I might just be reading them wrong. Hopefully I'm not.

"I actually have someone to meet." I reply and Owen arcs a brow.

"The other guy?" he asks. I cough, dropping my gaze and shifting uncomfortably when I realize Ian obviously told them, of course he did, he's obviously close with his dads.

"Owen," Haiden warns and elbows Owen in the side. I shake my head though, scratching the back of my neck.

"No, actually. It's my friend, she needs to talk to me." I reply, shifting uncomfortably.

"We will make this quick, then." Haiden assures. I wait a minute for him to continue and look up when Haiden doesn't start.

"Look Levy, you're an idiot." Owen drawls and Haiden elbows him in the side again so he clears his throat. "But you help Ian. You made him happier than I, well we, have seen him in quite a while. Then you two broke up, and Ian got bad again. He would hardly eat unless we made him, he was constantly blaring heavy metal and would barely talk to us.

"He was reverting back to the person he was after his ex took advantage of him. Look, my point is Ian needs you. He's a better person when he's around you, you make him happy, more like his old self. If you don't want to have a part in his life anymore, and you're just here because you feel guilty for him, then get the hell out of my house. But if you really care for him, then feel free to come over anytime you want. We would be glad to have you over." Owen finishes and I stare between the two in confusion. I open my mouth to speak but Owen cuts me a stern glare before continuing.

"And as long as Ian is happy, we don't care what kind of arrangement you have with him and the other guy. We want him to be happy, and you make him happy." Owen says, obviously a bit begrudgingly. I open my mouth to thank them, or something, but I can't seem to speak. I don't even know what to say, a simple thank you hardly seems fitting.

"I uh, thank you." I mumble and the two nod.

"Now you should go ahead and attend to your friend." Haiden states, obviously dismissing me without it seeming rude. I nod and leave the living room. I walk through the hall, out the front door, and to my car where I numbly drive to the park Lydia loves. I just can't believe everything seems to be working itself out, or starting to work itself out. Ian is talking to me, his dads don't want to kill me, and things are great with Jer.

I park in an empty spot, realizing since it is a weekend that there's a party going on. I get out and lock my car before looking around. I don't see Lydia so I slowly make my way across the large expanse of green grass, looking around for her. I nearly walk right past her because rather than having her hair dyed some bright, unnatural color, it's her natural dark, almost chocolate brown that she insists looks like shit.

I take a seat next to her on the green wooden bench and put my arm around her shoulders. She doesn't say anything in greeting and instead leans into my arms.

"What happened?" I ask after a while.

"Victoria and I were kissing and my mom walked in, freaked out then and my mom got mad at me. She told me she's sending me to some church camp for summer to "fix" me." She explains, sniffling as she does.

"Oh God, I'm so sorry. We'll figure this out." I assure, trying to think of something so she doesn't have to go.

"Thanks, Lev." She mumbles. I nod and rub her shoulders soothingly while she starts to cry into my chest. I don't comment though, I just continue to soothe her as best as I can.

"Do you want to stay the night? We can play games, watch movies and binge eat ice cream." I offer. She pulls away and nods, wiping her nose and eyes.

"That would be nice." She replies with a sniffle.

"Okay, come on." I urge, standing up and offering her my hand. She takes it and I lead her across the green grass, dodging some little kids playing tag, to my car. I open the passenger's door for her to get in, closing it before I get in the driver's seat and start the car. I carefully back out of the parking space and head towards my house.

I park next to Dad's car and get out of the car with Lydia, leading her across my yard to the door. I open the door, letting us in and go inside.

"Mom, Dad, I'm home and Lydia's going to stay the night." I call out, assuming they're in the house somewhere. I lead Lydia up the stairs, into my room after getting some ice cream and soda. Lydia lies down on the bed with the snacks while I move to my stack of DVDs, along with a few tapes I couldn't part with.

"What do you want to watch?" I ask, looking over all the titles on the cases.

"I want to watch 101 Dalmatians." She replies as she opens the cookie dough ice cream. I nod and carefully remove the tape from the stack before I slide it in my VCR. I turn on my TV, turn off the lights, and join Lydia on the bed.

I quickly text Ian, telling him I won't be back tonight, hoping he'll be okay. But then I realize this is Ian, he's stronger than his dads, and even I, think he is. He'll be okay. So I turn my phone to silent and enjoy my time with Lydia while we both ignore our problems for the time being.

The rest of the night we eat pizza my parents ordered for us, ice cream and drink a ton of soda while we watch a ton of movies. We laugh and joke around, avoiding the subject of how Lydia is going to avoid the camp until we fall asleep during The Long, Long Trailer.

~ ~ ~

I wake up to the sound of sirens. I open my eyes as I let out a groan, realizing at some point in the night Lydia had stolen all the blankets, kicked them off the bed, and used me as her personal heater. I sigh, glancing down at Lydia whose head is resting on my chest while her arms hug me in a crushing grip. I won't be surprised if I end up with bruises from her tight grasp around my torso.

"Lydia," I call, pulling one of my arms out of her crushing embrace to shake her a bit.

"Leave me alone if you want to live." She growls. I laugh but stop with a huff when she removes one of her arms from around my chest to punch me in the side.

"Ow, okay, jeez. Just let go, I have to pee." I mumble, pushing her away from me when I realize she fell back to sleep. I roll my eyes and manage to get out of bed without her killing me so I go into my bathroom to relieve my bladder. I flush, wash my hands and run a hand through my hair before going back into my room where Lydia is still snoring. Only now she's sprawled out on my bed, drooling on my pillow.

I shake my head and check my phone to make sure no one messaged me. I don't have any new messages so I toss it back on the dresser and leave my room. I go down the stairs into the kitchen where Mom's making scrambled eggs with bacon and toast.

"Smells good." I note, moving to the coffee pot full of fresh coffee. I pour some into a black mug and go to the fridge to pour some milk in, making the black liquid turn into a hazy toffee color. I take a seat at the small black wood table, sipping my coffee while Mom makes me a plate. She sets the plate of breakfast in front of me with a fork.

"Where is Lydia?" she asks, making another plate for herself. I assume Dad left already to go to work so I assume the plate is for Lydia, or herself.

"Lydia is right here." Lydia states, moving across the kitchen like a zombie to open the fridge. She pours herself a glass of orange juice as she claims it tastes better than coffee and wakes her up faster.

"Oh good, just in time. Here you go, hon." Mom sets the next plate full of eggs, bacon and toast in front of Lydia who nods her appreciation.

"Thank you. Sheryl." Lydia says but doesn't start eating, obviously with great difficulty on her part. I realize she's probably waiting for Mom so we can say grace, ever the polite little being. Whilst I on the other hand don't bother to wait because honestly I doubt God would care if I eat before thanking Him, obviously he knows how hungry I am and the last thing I want to do is wait any longer to eat.

Lydia rolls her eyes at me and I shrug. Mom doesn't seem bothered by my impatience, and instead sits down with her own plate before she bows her head with Lydia to say grace. They both finish with the prayer and say a collective "amen" then start eating. It's quiet for a while save for the clinking of the silver spoons on the brown ceramic plates until Mom breaks the silence.

"So Lydia, how is your Mom? I haven't spoken with her in quite a while." Mom adds thoughtfully, taking a drink from her glass of water.

"Oh she's," she stops and I can tell she's holding back an insult directed to her mom. I know Lydia loves her mom, but she crossed a line by threatening to send Lydia to a Jesus camp to fix something that isn't even a problem. "Fine." Lydia replies, taking a large drink from her orange juice.

"Oh good, I'll have to talk to her later today after church." Mom says. Then it's silent again until we finish eating. The two of us put our plates in the sink before moving up to my room, thanking Mom on the way.

"So what are we going to do?" I ask, looking around my room, once clean but now cluttered with DVD cases, empty cans of soda, and an empty tub of cookie dough ice cream.

"Clean your room?" she offers. I roll my eyes but nod, moving to pick up all the empty cans and tub of ice cream while Lydia stacks the DVDs in their perspective places. I go to the kitchen to throw everything away and go back to my room where she's making my bed. She sits down on it before looking around.

"Your phone buzzed, and I hope you don't mind but I'm going to go talk to Victoria. She was kind of freaked out yesterday, she didn't want to leave but, well, my mom." She says and I nod, not bothering to ask what about her mom because that's enough explanation. I check my phone, smiling slightly at the good morning message from Jer.

"Yeah, I don't mind. I actually have to talk to someone anyway." I reply, leaving out who I plan to talk to.

"Okay, well I'll talk to you later. Thanks for being here with me, Lev." She stands and pulls me into a tight hug.

"You don't have to thank me, Lyd. That's what friends are for." I reply. She pulls away and gathers her things before leaving my room. I sigh and flop down on my bed, texting Ian to tell him I'm coming over in a few minutes. I get changed, fix my hair, and gather my things before I leave the room, hoping Ian is feeling better today.

Chapter Twenty-Three

{ Chapter Twenty-Three}

I go up to the door and knock when I get to Ian's house. Haiden answers with a bright smile and motions me into the house.

"Levy, I wasn't expecting you. Ian is up in his room." He adds after closing the front door and turning the lock. I take a step towards the hall but glance at Haiden, trying to read from his face if everything is okay. Considering he answered the door smiling, I assume everything is okay. He also looks fine, a bit happier than he was yesterday for sure. So I nod with a smile of my own and walk through the familiar hallway.

Passing white walls and family photos, along with the living room where Owen is watching some kind of romance film. I walk up the stairs and down the next hall, stopping at Ian's door. I open it without bothering to knock and bite my lip.

Ian is once again at his desk, typing on his computer quickly with earbuds in to drown out every other noise. I close the door behind me and move across the room, getting a sense of deja vu when I hear the distinct sound of heavy metal coming through his earbuds.

I move behind him and tap him on the shoulder, still unsure if it would be okay to wrap my arms around him like I want to. He jumps in surprise, yanking his earbuds out and turning in his chair. His eyes brighten when he registers that it's just me and I smile.

"Hey," I greet and he grins, jumping out of his chair to hug me.

"Hey," he echos in greeting. I smile, holding him tightly to me and resting my chin on his head.

"Ian, I...we need to talk, baby." I state, pulling away to look at him. He looks at me with curious and nervous gray eyes.

"About what?" he asks nervously. I smile wanly at that, hoping he doesn't get upset.

"About us." I reply and clear my throat, dropping my eyes. "You, me, and Jer." I add and he stiffens though I don't expect anything less.

"Okay." He says with a nod after a moment of silence. I look around and lean down to kiss his temple lightly.

"Come on, let's go to the park." I say. I don't want to talk to him in his room, not that I don't like it because it's really nice but I don't want to talk about our relationship in the room where his last relationship was destroyed.

He tilts his head to the side in confusion but nods anyway and moves to pull his shoes on, grabbing his wallet and phone as well. I take his hand, leading him out his room, through the hall and down the stairs past the living room.

"I'll be back," he calls when we're halfway to the front door. I unlock the front door, open it and we slip out as Haiden tells us to be back before midnight. I walk across the grass to my blue Camaro parked at the curb, while Ian seems to take the stone path to the driveway, avoiding the grass.

I open the passenger's door for him and he slides in so I close the door, moving to the driver's door. I get in, close the door and turn the key, making the car start up with ease. I pull away from the curb and head to the park that's about a mile from his house. I park in an empty spot and we get out, walking to the gazebo close to the play structure in the middle of the park.

I look around the less than pristine gazebo, catching sight of numerous spots where the eggshell white yellow is chipped, revealing the aged brown wood beneath. I walk over to the railing facing the brightly colored play structure where kids are running around and laughing. Ian takes a spot next to me but I keep my eyes on the play structure.

"I don't want you to feel forced into anything." I state and continue before he can say anything in response. "If you don't want to be in this relationship, if it makes you uncomfortable in any way, I don't want you to feel like you have to stay with me. I want you to be happy, even if that means I won't have you."

"Levy," he starts and I finally tear my eyes from the play structure to look at him.

"I want you to be happy, Ian." I state, taking his hand and giving it a squeeze.

"I know, and I know what will make me happy." He says seriously, looking into my eyes. I realize when I search his eyes that he's so much stronger than I give him credit for, he's not some fragile vase that's going to break into a million pieces at the slightest touch. It makes me happy to know he's strong, even if he doesn't act like it.

"What will make you happy?" I ask at last. He takes my other hand in his and pulls me closer, looking up at me as he's a little shorter than me.

"You. You'll make me happy, Levy. You're not forcing me to do anything, and I appreciate that so much. I love you and I'm sure we can make it work. I don't want to loose you, I don't want to look back in thirty years and wish I had stayed with you. I want to look at you in thirty years and be happy that I chose to be with you." He explains, standing on his tip toes to kiss me chastely.

When he pulls back I realize my eyes had begun to water so I quickly look away and clear my throat, attempting to compose myself. When I'm sure that I won't begin to cry I turn back to Ian and smile.

"I'm happy to hear that." I reply, my voice cracking a bit but I ignore it. He smiles and pulls me to the center of the gazebo, catching me by surprise. He wordlessly puts his right hand on my waist and moves our left hands out, positioning us in a dancing pose.

"You want to dance?" I ask, looking around for any parents or guardians who may have a fit about us filling their child's mind with filthy ideas. It wouldn't surprise me, I know not everyone in the town could possibly be okay with it, there's always some bigot out there.

"Why not?" he asks, taking a step closer and I instinctively take one step back, remembering when I was younger and Mom would attempt to teach me how to slow dance. I laugh and dance around the gazebo with him, even twirling him before dipping him. He looses it at that point, laughing and making me drop him when he looses his footing. Of course, he manages to pull me down with him by latching onto my arm.

I fall on top of him, causing him to huff from the sudden weight of my body on his but he continues to laugh breathlessly.

"Ugh," I groan but I'm laughing as well. I push myself off him to sit on the dusty worn wood floor of the gazebo and he does the same as he begins to regain his composure. I smile at that, happy to see Ian smile and laugh so much.

"See? That was fun." Ian states, standing up and dusting off his clothes before extending a hand out to me. I take it and he helps me up and helps me get all the dust off my clothes.

"So it was." I reply with a grin. We're silent and I bite my lip as I get an idea. "Do you want to have lunch and meet Jer?"

He looks at me in surprise and seems to think about it for a few minutes. I shift from foot to foot, hoping he says yes. At last he nods slowly, nervous-ly.

"Okay." He agrees. I smile and pull my phone out to ask Jer if he can come to lunch.

"Where would you like to eat?" I ask after I put my phone back into my back pocket. I entwine our fingers and lead him down the steps, across the green grass back to my car.

"Oh, there's this place on Eighth that has really good sandwiches. Can we go there?" I nod and drop his hand to get to my door. My eyes widen and I let out a choked sound, surprising Ian. He moves over to me quickly and grabs my wrist.

"Are you okay? What's wrong?" he questions worriedly and I wordlessly motion to the car. He stares at it in confusion while I stare at it in horror.

"Someone scratched her beautiful paint." I state, staring at the scratch marring her previously perfect blue paint.

"What? Wait, that?" he points at the scratch. "It's tiny. A surface scratch actually." He adds with an arced brow.

"Someone is going to pay." I threaten, ignoring Ian's assurance and looking around for the person who committed this crime.

"Wow," he sighs, dropping my hand and taking my keys out of my pocket. "It's a car, you can easily get it fixed. It'll be pretty cheap too, Owen can actually do it." He adds and unlocks the door before sliding into the driver's seat. I snap out of my horrified state to look at Ian, who already has the door closed. I try to open it but it's locked so I sigh and reluctantly get in the passenger's seat.

"Why does everyone insist on driving my car? She's mine, I should be the only one driving her." I grumble, putting my seat belt on while Ian pulls out of the parking spot.

"I'm not sure you know where the place is so why not drive rather than try to give you directions? That's okay, right? 'Cause I'll pull over if you don't want me to drive." He adds, nervousness entering his voice.

"No, it's okay. I trust you won't hurt her anymore than she's already been." I add in exasperation before smiling and reaching over to take one of his hands in mine, lacing our fingers. The drive is silent as he drives across town to a small little diner tucked between two other buildings. He parks in front of the diner and we get out after I tell Jer where to meet us.

We go in and take a seat, waiting for a waiter to give us a menu. I look around at the all-American type restaurant with checkered tables and paintings meant to be realistic in style. My eyes move from the paintings back to Ian who's looking at a painting of the diner positioned above our table.

"When will he be here?" he asks nervously and I shrug, not really knowing.

"Probably in a few minutes, he doesn't live too far from here." I add, glancing at my phone to see Jer said he would be here in a few. I look back to Ian and reach over to take his hand in reassurance because he's begun to fidget.

"It's going to be okay," I assure though I don't really know that. What if they don't get along? What if this is too much for Ian? Or Jer realizes he can't do this? But I don't voice those concerns, instead I smile reassuringly at Ian.

"I hope so," he mumbles. I open my mouth to say something else but the door opens and Jer walks in. My eyes move to him, taking in his light gray shirt under his heavy leather jacket, black jeans with a chain attached and black combat boots with his golden blond hair perfectly styled. He catches my eyes and an easy smile finds its way on his lips as he moves across the diner to our table, taking a seat.

"Hey, I'm Jeremiah, you must be Ian." Jer says, extending his hand to Ian. I let go of Ian's hand so he can reach out and take Jer's, shaking it with a nod.

"Yep, that's me. Well, I mean, you probably knew that though. Unless you didn't know Levy, that would be more awkward than my awkward babbling." Ian replies before groaning, dropping his head as pink tinges his cheeks. I cough to disguise my laughter while Jer silently shakes with laughter.

"So you go to private school?" Jer asks, obviously moving the conversation so Ian won't feel as embarrassed. Ian looks back at Jer after shrugging.

"Yeah, it's not as bad as everyone makes it seem though. The worst part is the uniforms, and they're a bit more strict than public school, but I don't mind." He explains calmly while Jer nods.

A waitress drops off three menus, asking for our drink orders before Jer can respond to Ian's reply. We all put in our drink orders and she leaves us, allowing Jer to reply.

"I went to a private school through high school, it wasn't bad, just not fun." He adds with a shrug and Ian nods. The table falls silent and Ian clears his throat, causing me to jump slightly in surprise while Ian drops his eyes.

"I don't know if I'll be able to trust you," he mumbles, glancing at me and biting his lip. "Either of you." He adds and I open my mouth to assure him he can trust both of us but he speaks before I can.

"I'm going to go to the bathroom." He states and I nod numbly while he gets up and moves quickly to the bathroom. I move to follow him, worried that he's upset but Jer reaches out to place his hand on top of mine.

"Stay, I'll check on him." He adds with a small smile. I nod reluctantly before he gets up to follow Ian. Leaving me to hope everything is okay, but I can't be sure.

Chapter Twenty-Four

<hr>

{ Chapter Twenty-Four}

The waitress drops off the drinks and asks if I want to order yet but I tell her to give me a minute so Jer and Ian can order too. After a few minutes, no sign of either of them, I start to get more nervous. What if Ian is freaking out? Or if they're fighting. I want to go in to see if they're okay, and I'm about to. I pocket my phone and grab Jer's wallet in case someone tries to take it, and start to stand until the bathroom door opens. I sit back down, putting Jer's wallet back while the two emerge from the bathroom.

I scan both of them for any signs that something is wrong, but I can't find anything out of the ordinary. In fact, Ian looks more relaxed than he has been since we got here. I relax at that, sighing in relief. They both take their seats and the waitress comes back to take our orders.

"Is everything okay?" I ask, not really aiming it at either one of them in particular, just hoping one of them will answer. Jer's eyes move to Ian whose eyes find mine.

"Yeah." Ian replies with a smile, his gray eyes bright with that familiar light. My eyes move to Jer who lifts his two fingers to his lips in a motion one would do to take a drag off a cigarette, making me realize he probably wants one.

The waitress comes back to get our orders and we all give her our individual orders. When she skips away my eyes move to Ian, still worried about him. What I said at the park was completely true, I don't want him to feel forced into anything. I want him to trust us, and hopefully over time we can build that trust if he really wants this.

"This can be dangerous." I blurt, moving my eyes from Ian to Jer, addressing both of them. Ian arcs his brow in confusion while Jer drops his eyes to inspect his tattoo.

"I know," Jer is the first to speak, lifting his fingers to his lips again but keeping his golden eyes on his thick black cross poking out of his leather jacket on his right hand.

"What do you mean?" Ian asks seriously and I look into his near-white gray eyes. Images of us coming out to just the town flash through my mind; they would be sickened, I know it. It's not that the town isn't open to new things, but I don't know if everyone-or even the majority of everyone-would be open to this kind of relationship. Almost everyone has it set in their minds that monogamy is the only correct relationship, the only type of relationship that's real.

They would be sickened. They could hurt us; Jer, Ian. Images of Ian coming to me with bruises, especially considering he's in a private Catholic school, flash through my mind. What if they get hurt? It would be my fault, I'm the one who's bringing us together. If they get hurt because of this I would never forgive myself.

"You could get hurt," I reply to Ian's question. "You could get hurt because of me. This isn't just a matter of some people not thinking this is right, this is a matter of God only knows how many people thinking this is wrong.

We'd be shunned, harassed, loose friends. Are you ready for that? Are you ready to possibly loose all your friends? Get hurt?" I ask near hysteria because the weight of all this is beginning to weigh down on me.

"Levy," Jer starts in a calm voice.

"And you, my mom might hate you. You could go out of business. Get hurt." I add, biting my lip hard to stay in this moment and not get lost in all the possible outcomes. Jer reaches out and takes my hand in his gently, making my eyes snap from the table to him then to Ian when his hand takes my free one.

"Calm down," Jer soothes, running his thumb against the top of my hand in soothing circles. Ian locks our fingers and offers me a smile.

"I know people may disapprove, but I'm not as fragile as you think I am. If someone tries to hurt me, I can and will defend myself. I won't be a victim again." He adds the last part lowly. My heart clenches at that and I squeeze his fingers comfortingly. Jer's eyes look to me in confusion, no doubt wondering what Ian meant because I haven't told anyone what happened to Ian. It's his choice to tell people, I have no right to tell anyone about his past. He'll tell Jer in due time if he wants to.

"We're going to be okay, love. We can take whatever backlash we receive." Jer adds, not voicing his obvious confusion over Ian's earlier statement.

"I don't want you to get hurt." I reply, speaking to both of them.

"We won't." They say simultaneously. My eyes dart between them, reading their relaxed but serious expressions.

"You don't know that." I mutter, dropping my eyes. I know I want to be with them, I love them so much, but I don't want to do something that will get them hurt. I don't want to take that risk unless they're both sure. "You're not giving us much credit," Ian states and I sigh.

"I'm scared." I reply honestly.

"We can make this work, love, no one has to get hurt." Jer assures and I open my mouth to reply but close it. I don't know how to reply to that. I know he's right, we can make this work and I'm probably getting worked up over nothing, but at the same time there may be a reason to be worked up.

The waitress drops our food off, giving me a distraction from thinking about all this. I pick up my turkey sandwich and take a bite, savoring the smoky flavor. We all eat in silence, each lost in our own thoughts. Ian seems to finish his sandwich first, followed by me then Jer. The waitress drops off the check and I reach for it as does Jer, Ian probably knows there's no use trying to pay, unlike Jer.

"I'm paying," I state, taking the check but Jer doesn't let go.

"I'll pay, love." Jer replies, pulling the check to himself but I stare flatly at him.

"I invited you, I should pay." I argue, yanking the check back towards myself.

"I decided to come and order food, I planned to pay." he argues.

"I don't work hard for my money." I add. It's true, I don't work for my money, Mom and Dad just want me to do well in school and if I do I can keep my credit card as long as I don't go crazy.

"I have more money than you." He replies. I notice Ian is shaking with silent laughter, shaking his head at the exchange.

"I..." I trail, thinking as fast as I can. "I should pay."

"I'm older." He replies and I open my mouth but close it when the black leather book holding our check is pulled out of both our grasps.

"Neither of you are paying." Ian deadpans, pulling his wallet out of his pocket before getting up to go pay the bill. I stare after him, dumbfounded.

"I wanted to pay," I state sadly, watching Ian hand the hostess a twenty before coming back to the table. "I was going to pay," I inform Ian but Jer laughs.

"He thinks he was going to pay." He says, correcting me.

"It's fine, my dads give me a large allowance and if I let you guys continue we would be here all day." Ian replies. I drop my head but smile at Ian anyway, standing up so we can leave.

"Do you guys want to go anywhere?" I ask, stretching a bit while Ian stands, Jer following. Ian's eyes brighten and his lips twitch in a smile.

"Can we go to the beach?" he asks in excitement and I look at the large retro red and black clock with white numbers on the wall across the room, wondering if we would have time.

"I think we can manage that." I reply with a smile and Ian's eyes lighten up. I look to Jer who's smiling at Ian's excitement. "Can you drive? I don't want to get sand in my car." I explain, shuddering at the mere thought.

"Of course, do you want to drop your car off at your house? Or we could drop it at mine since it's closer. Or the office." My eyes widen at the last part and he arcs a brow.

"I am not leaving my baby at your office unattended. She could be hurt...again." I add, cringing at the memory of the scratch someone left on her beautiful paint. Jer looks to Ian in confusion while Ian rolls his eyes in exasperation.

"Someone scratched his car, it's just a surface scratch though. I tried to tell him it was nothing to worry about, that my dad can buff it out, but I don't know if he was listening. " Ian explains. Jer nods, looking back to me.

"You can park it at my house then, it'll be safe and it's closer than yours." He assures but I know what he's not adding.

It's more convenient to leave it at his because if I drop my car off at my house Mom and Dad are going to ask a hundred questions as to why I'm not driving it. And since Lydia doesn't have her license while Jess doesn't have a car, it wouldn't make sense to tell them I'm with Lydia or Jess. It's less of a hassle to drop it off at his house.

We all leave the diner and out to the cars. Ian, surprisingly, moves to the passenger's side door of Jer's black 4Runner. I don't say anything though and instead move to my own driver's door, sliding in and pulling out after Jer. I follow behind him back to his house and pull into his familiar cement driveway while he parks at the curb. I get out, looking at my car longingly before patting it.

"You'll be okay," I assure, petting the pretty blue paint before locking her up and walking towards Jer's truck. I slide into the back passenger's seat and move up to drape my arms on Ian, feeling his strong abdomen under my fingers through his gray shirt.

"Were you just talking to your car?" Jer asks in confusion, pulling away from the curb and driving towards the highway that will lead us to the closest beach.

"Yes, do you have a problem with that?" I demand a bit dramatically, resting my head against the back of Ian's polyester headrest to look at Jer's profile. He shakes his head, chuckling lightly but doesn't respond, instead focuses on the road. My eyes move to Ian as I rub small circles on his chest soothingly while he closes his eyes.

I don't know when it happened but at some point I realize he fell asleep, and despite the fact that if he sleeps he'll probably have a worse time getting to sleep tonight, I don't have the heart to wake him. I lift my left hand to run through his soft dark hair, letting the silky strands fall through my fingers with ease.

"He fell asleep fast," Jer notes and I nod, continuing to run my fingers through his hair.

"He doesn't sleep well at night, and I guess he relaxes enough around me to sleep." I half explain, keeping a close eye on the road because I easily get car sick.

"Why do you suppose he wanted to go to the beach?" Jer questions. I shrug, admittedly I'm curious too.

"Maybe he was just in the mood for it." I offer, savoring the feel of Ian's soft hair. Jer doesn't respond to that, instead he continues to drive down the highway, passing cars.

He moves lanes and turns his blinker on to merge into another lane. He pulls off the off ramp that will lead to the road that will lead to the beach. We pass empty fields with iceberg plants and purple flowers before Jer reaches the parking lot of the beach. Jer parks in an empty spot next to a monstrosity of a truck that I'm sure costs more to fill up per day than Jer makes off bulk sale. I roll my eyes at the comparison, realizing I spent way too much time talking about marketing and money with Jer for the project.

"Ian," I call but I don't stop running my fingers through his hair. He sighs and his eyes open, looking around as he blinks.

"We're here," Ian mumbles and I laugh.

"I know. Come on, babe, let's walk on the beach." I offer, sliding out of the truck. Ian follows, stepping out and leaning against the closed door as he wakes up a bit more. Jer gets out and walks over to us, locking his fingers with mine.

"We can take our shoes off and put them in the back." Jer offers and we nod, moving to the back of the truck. We take our shoes off, putting all our wallets and electronics-watches and phones-in the back before Jer locks it. We move across the hard pavement into the sand and walk towards the water.

I notice Ian breathes in deeply, looking around before a grin appears on his face. He turns to me, grabbing my hand and lacing our fingers, not looking tired in the least.

"Come on," he urges, dropping my hand and running towards the water. I laugh, leaning against Jer as Ian runs to the water. I look up at Jer and kiss him lightly with a smile.

"You coming?" I question and he shakes his head, tipping my head up with his fingers to kiss me.

"Go on, I'll be right here." He assures. I nod and make my way through the soft warm sand to where Ian is waiting, the waves barely missing him. He looks over at my approach and smiles, taking my hand and leading me closer to the water.

"I don't want to get wet." I warn.

"Oh don't worry, you won't get wet." He waves off, walking slower once we get to the hard packed cold sand. We walk close to the water, but not close enough to get wet which I'm grateful for. I look over to Jer who took a seat in the sand not too far from us, smiling at us.

"Lev, look, I found a sand dollar." Ian calls, bending down to wipe at the sand. I bend down on my hunches next to him to look at what he's wiping at but I don't see anything.

"Wait, where?" I ask in confusion. Then I feel it. Freezing cold water splashes me up to my waist and I gasp, unable to move while Ian laughs.

"I'm sorry, I had to." Ian gasps out, pushing me back to the sand and I groan.

"Why," I whine, looking up at him when he leans over me. He smiles, his gray eyes holding that light that makes a smile find its way onto my lips.

"It was just too easy." He explains, leaning in closer as he keeps himself propped above me with his hands in the cold packed sand. I watch him curiously and he drops down further to kiss me.

I smile against his lips while his move against mine roughly. I move my hands up up his shirt but he stiffens under my hands, pulling them out of his shirt with his right hand. I plan to ask if he's okay but then a large wave of ice cold water splashes over us and all thoughts of lust are washed away.

"Ugh," I groan while Ian pulls away, dropping his head on my shoulder as he laughs. "You think this is funny?" I probe, pulling his now wet hair so he's looking up at me.

"A bit."

"I have sand in places I didn't know it would be possible to get sand and I'm frozen." I deadpan but he just continues to smile brightly, the light in his eyes never wavering. He looks so happy, it makes me break my composure and smile.

"Alright, come on, we can get up and you can go complain to Jer about how mean I am." Ian mocks, pushing himself off me and onto his feat before extending his hand to me. I take it and he helps me up, attempting to wipe some of the sand off my clothes but it doesn't help much.

"Come on," Ian coaxes, taking my hand so I won't continue to attempt to wipe the sand off my clothes. We walk back to where Jer is, crossing from packed wet sand to damp loose sand until we reach the dry sand. Jer looks us over and laughs.

"You got wet," he states. I pout, pushing Ian and moving behind Jer.

"He tricked me." I whine, pointing my finger at Ian who's snickering.

"I saw, it was amusing." Jer says and turns to me, wrapping his arms around my shoulders. "Come on, we'll take a walk and you can dry off." Jer offers, reaching out to take Ian's hand.

I smile at that and we walk down the beach. We walk through the sand, moving from one end of the beach to the next as the sun slowly moves further down the sky, and everything is easy. We don't have to worry about anything right now, we can talk about stuff with no meaning, we don't have to worry about reality. It's amazing, I don't want it to end.

But as the sun descends further, indicating the day is over, I know we have to go back to reality. We walk back to the truck where me and Ian attempt to get most of the sand off our clothes. Most of it comes off easily now that it's dry but I can still feel it on my body under my clothes. I ignore it though and slide into the back with Ian while Jer slides into the driver's seat.

I rest my head against the window, tired from today. I close my eyes and start to drift off when I feel arms wrap around my arm followed by Ian's head resting against my shoulder.

"Thank you, Levy. This was perfect." He mumbles tiredly and I smile, nodding slightly.

"Anytime, babe." I reply softly before my eyes shut. I don't fall asleep though, I force myself to stay up so I can get some sleep tonight. I let Ian sleep though, I know he won't sleep tonight either way unless he takes a sleeping pill which he seems so prone to doing.

The ride back to town seems faster than it did coming to the beach. I give Jer directions to Ian's house and he parks at the curb in front of Ian's house. I open my mouth to wake Ian, but when I look down at him, I can't.

"Jer, help me get him out of the car. I don't want to wake him." I add, carefully moving him so I can slide out of the truck. Jer gets out and reaches in to carefully take Ian in his arms before handing him to me.

"You got him?" Jer asks quietly and I nod with a grateful smile.

"I have him. I'll be right back, I'm going to attempt to get him in bed without waking him." I add and Jer nods, reaching out to move a stray hair from Ian's face.

"Good luck, love." He replies before getting back into the truck. I carefully walk across the greening grass to Ian's front door. I knock on it carefully with my foot, hoping Haiden or Owen-Haiden-will answer the door. Owen answers and I sigh when his eyes move from me to Ian's unconscious form.

"Before you freak out, he's fine. He just fell asleep in the car and I didn't want to wake him because he doesn't sleep well." I interrupt him before he can say anything, and I know he was about to. He puffs up his chest, looking at me with no emotion before moving aside to let me in.

"Come on." Owen mutters so I carefully move into the house. I hear Owen close the door as I make my way up the stairs. I reach Ian's open door and carefully place Ian on his bed. I pull his shirt off and carefully take his pants off, leaving him in his black boxers. Then I pull his fluffy comforter over his sleeping form and lean down to kiss him on the lips gently.

"I love you, baby. Sleep well." I whisper though I know he's going to wake up sometime during the night. I leave his room, taking two steps at a time before I walk through the hall. To my surprise I make it out the door without either of Ian's dads confronting me.

I walk across the lawn to the passenger's door of Jer's car and get in. He glances over at me, taking my hand in one of his and lacing our fingers together.

"Did he wake up?" he asks and I shake my head, yawning as I rest my head on his arm.

"He will later, but for now he's sleeping." I mumble. I imagine Jer nods but I can't be sure as I close my eyes, waiting to get to Jer's house so I can go home. Though, the thought of driving makes me groan.

"I don't think I can drive." I state, yawning involuntarily as if to prove my point. "Can you just drop me off? I can pick up my car tomorrow." I add.

"Yeah of course. If you need a ride tomorrow tell me, I'll pick you up." He replies. I nod but don't say anything as he continues driving. He stops in front of my house and I lean over to kiss him on the cheek. He smiles, turns his head and grabs my chin to kiss me on the lips.

"I'll see you tomorrow." I say, pulling back with a tired smile.

"I'll see you tomorrow, love." He replies. I get out and lean into the car for a minute.

"I love you," I say before I close the door and make my way up to my door. I slip into the house and after taking a short hot shower I slide into bed. I don't bother to put anything on and instead snuggle into my soft sheets, thinking of the great day as I fall asleep, not ready for Monday.

~~ The extra scene for this chapter (which shows what happened between Ian and Jer) can be found in my book on my profile called Experience The Rainbow, the one shot is called Ian & Jer -MMB Chapter 24.

Here's the link: https://www.wattpad.com/250465228-experience-the-rainbow-lgbt%2B-one-shots-ian-jer-mmb

The link is also an external link on this chapter. If you have any problems locating it, please leave a comment or PM me so I can send you a clickable link. :) ~~

Chapter Twenty-Five

Monday.

I didn't know a single day could be so horrible. It's not like someone wakes up on Wednesday and hates it already, but Monday is somehow horrible. It's not like I even hate Monday, I'm just exhausted. I didn't get a lot of sleep last night despite going to sleep nine hours ago, because the sleep I did get was riddled with nightmares. Nightmares of the worst scenarios if people find out about my relationship with Ian and Jer, our relationship; about the worst way my parents could react.

The nightmares had me waking up nearly every hour, or so it felt. It was horrid and adding school to the exhaustion does not help.

I send a text to Lydia, telling her I can't pick her up for school and I'll explain later. I stumble out of bed, falling to my hard floor with a grunt before sitting up and running my fingers through my hair.

I get up, stumbling over to my dresser to pull out a clean black shirt. I glance around the room and pick up a pair of blue jeans I know are clean from the ground before pulling them on, not bothering with boxers today.

I slide my phone in my pocket, grabbing my wallet from the nightstand along with my keys before I leave my room. Since I have to walk to school I skip breakfast and just walk out the front door. I turn check my phone as I make my way down the street, not seeing any new messages so I stuff it back in my pocket.

The walk is incredibly boring, making me wonder why anyone would just go out into nature for fun. There's nothing to do, the only good thing to look at is the blooming colorful spring flowers and green trees but those get boring after a while. Plus it's way too quiet, and this is just going down a couple streets that don't tend to be busy, I couldn't imagine going into the forest or something. I would be so bored.

I walk into the school building, thankful I made it in time to grab my stuff before class. I walk to my locker and Lydia is waiting for me with a bored expression until she sees me.

"Levy, you look horrible." She notes, scanning me from head to toe.

"Thanks Lyd, I can always count on your honesty." I drawl sarcastically, opening my locker to grab what I'll need for my first class.

"Why couldn't you give me a ride? I had to ask my mom and things are kind of awkward around her right now." She adds and I look over at her, taking in her bright pink hair and unnaturally green contacts. It makes me happy to see her like this again, it means she's feeling better.

"I don't have my car." I reply as the bell rings and I lean over to kiss her cheek. "I'll tell you everything during lunch." I interrupt before she can ask about my lack of vehicle because I know she wants to ask.

I go to first period and yawn, dropping my head to the cold surface of the table because this is an easy class so I don't need to pay attention. I don't let myself fall asleep though because I know if I do I won't be able to wake up. The teacher starts the lecture, something about bugs or maybe a war. I have no idea, I couldn't be bothered to pay any mind to it.

~ ~ ~

I slide into my seat for English, about to rest my head on the table but the teacher starts off by saying we're going to go over our grades for the project. So I keep my eyes open and focus on her boring monotone voice.

"While most of you did well with the paper part, I noticed some of you were quite lacking with your presentations. However, I will say that every one of you got a passing grade for this project despite the many flaws I noticed. Today I will pass back your paper with notes I made along with an evaluation sheet that breaks down the points by categories, it will show you which parts you got the most points for. When I call your name I want you to come up and collect your papers." She explains.

We nod and she starts calling out names. I zone out for a while until she calls out my name so I numbly go up to the front to take my papers from her. I don't dare look at the papers until I'm in my seat with them face down on my table. I bite my lip, suddenly nervous about my grade.

I quickly turn the paper to face me though, looking past my name and the class information to the actual points earned. My eyes widen when I see my points for the paper, I got full points and what more, the teacher actually put a smiley face with 'good job!' next to the paper grade. I didn't get full points on the presentation but I did get a passing grade, above passing in fact, so that's all that matters.

I scan through the actual paper for any notes but most of them aren't very in depth notes. Just some comments and questions that are answered in my paper. I sigh in relief at that and slip the papers into my English folder before droning out the class again, waiting for lunch.

I leave English, moving to my next class which is just as boring as the next. And finally, lunch comes. The previously desolate halls become packed with students, they crash into me as if I'm not even here but I don't bother getting mad at them. I simply stuff my books in my locker and move towards the lunchroom.

I spot Lydia and Jessica sitting at our usual spot so after I get some food I go to sit down. It's silent for a while at the table, though the room is filled with loud chatter. Finally I sigh, dropping my head to the cold metal table.

"I have something to tell you guys." I mumble, not bothering to pick my head up to look at them.

"What's wrong?" they ask at the same time and I bite my lip. I doubt they'll really care too much about the relationship, I'm pretty sure I made it clear when I told them about Ian what kind of relationship I was looking for so I trust them not to get mad and do something drastic, but it's still nerve wracking, and surreal.

"I got Ian back." I say at first and I hear them making weird noises of what I can only guess are joy. "And Jer." I add before clearing my throat. "We all worked everything out."

"Wait, what?" Lydia asks but I can't tell from her voice what she's feeling, if she's surprised or angry.

"We all worked it out." I repeat though I keep my voice to a low whisper in case someone is eavesdropping on us. The last thing I need is to be outed to the whole school, then word would get around all over town and we would all be screwed.

"Oh my gosh!" Jess squeals and I flinch from the high pitched noise. "That's so great, I'm so happy for you guys."

"I'm with Jess, I'm so happy you could work all this out. Wait so if everything is okay, why do you look the same as you did when Ian dumped you? And why don't you have your car?" Lydia asks and I yawn into the table.

"I couldn't sleep last night," I explain about the nightmares then everything that happened yesterday, explaining why I don't have my car.

"So you're going to see Jer again today?" Lydia probes and I can tell she's grinning.

"Yeah, that's the only way I'll get my car back. He's going to pick me up after school to take me to my car." I reply, finally lifting my head to look between the grinning girls. I lean back in my chair, frowning in confusion. "Why do you guys look so evil?"

"We're not evil," Jess whines, leaning across the table to smack me in the arm. I flinch but roll my eyes, dropping them to the table as I yawn again.

"How many more hours until school is over?" I ask wistfully as I poke at my burger.

"Three," Lydia replies and I groan.

"This is so boring. I can't wait till I graduate." I mutter. Then I remember the fact that I have to get a job after I graduate, or at least go to college. I shudder at the thought because I know college is going to be ten times worse than this, and this is already hell.

"I can't believe we're graduating in a month." Lydia says, seeming to ignore my statement, or the first part anyway.

"I know, it's so weird right?" Jess muses and I sigh. They look over at me before looking at each other and back to me.

"Your birthday is in a couple weeks." They say in creepy unison.

"I know." I mutter, recalling that Mom had started talking about it a few days ago, something about a big party.

"Oh! Are you guys going to prom?" Jess asks and I arc a brow. I haven't really thought of it but it is this month, in a matter of weeks. Of course, I would have to choose to go with Ian or Jer and I doubt either would want to go to prom. It's not that fun, just a bunch of teenagers trying to spike the punch and dance dirty while the teachers weren't watching. That's what it was like last year.

"I don't think so," I reply, looking at Lydia who shakes her head.

"I'm going out with Victoria that night." She replies so I turn to Jess.

"Why, are you going?" I ask in surprise. Jess is the last person I would expect to be at prom, she's more into academics and sports than romance. She's focused on her grades and has never, to date, gone to any of the school events or dances. Which means someone asked her and offered to pay for her ticket.

"Yeah, you know Brad?" she questions and my brows raise in surprise.

"Brad Hill?" I ask for confirmation and she nods with a big grin.

"He asked me Friday if I wanted to come. And since the teachers have been easing up on all the homework I decided to agree." She explains but I just continue to stare at her.

"Why Brad though?" I probe. I mean, Brad is nice but he's kind of a nerd. He spends a major amount of his time playing strategy based bored games with the computer geeks, yet he doesn't get great grades. He also has this weird mole under his nose that looks like a booger from far away, and odd orange curly hair. But I guess if Jess likes him, who am I to judge? At least she isn't going out with the Jan Hanson, the more popular guy who is known for being a jerk to his girlfriends.

"He's really nice." She replies automatically so I nod, not bothering to push the subject.

After lunch I go back to the hellish confines of those classrooms, listening to stuff I already knew and getting a stack of papers I don't want. Finally, after another three hours of this never ending nightmare, we're released. I take my stuff from my locker and make my way through the crowded halls, arriving at the front doors.

I leave the building and glance around before smiling when I see Jer's 4Runner parked in front by the curb. I walk over to it, sliding in when I make it to the passenger's door.

"Hey," I greet tiredly and Jer smiles.

"Hey, how was school?" he questions as he shifts to drive and starts the way towards his house.

"Hellish." I reply with another yawn as I close my eyes. I feel his hand rest on top of mine and I smile, lacing our fingers together. His cold rings rest comfortably against my skin and I sigh in content, frowning when we park.

"Do you want to come in and watch a movie?" Jer asks. I open my eyes and turn my head to the side to look at him before smiling.

"I'd love to." I reply. He smiles softly with a nod and we get out of the truck. We walk across the green grass to his front door that he opens up to me. I slip into the house, going to the couch in the living room where I take a seat. He follows suit after hanging his leather jacket on the coat hanger and putting a disc into the DVD player.

I move to lay my head in his lap and he starts running his fingers through my hair soothingly as he starts the movie. I attempt to keep my eyes open to watch the familiar movie about a woman who falls in love with this dance instructor who in all honesty isn't that attractive and he's kind of a jerk.

However, at some point my eyes close and don't open back up as I fall asleep while Jer runs his fingers through my hair, relaxing me.

Chapter Twenty-Six

{ Chapter Twenty-Six}

I wake up when Jer gets up and I open my tired eyes to look up at him. He smiles apologetically at me and wipes a strand of hair from my eyes.

"I didn't mean to wake you." He says and I wave him off with a yawn.

"What time is it?" I ask as I sit up and run a hand through my blond hair. He glances at his black watch on his left hand to check the time.

"Almost six." He replies and I nod.

"Okay, I'm going to get going then." I reply, knowing Mom is going to get mad if I'm not back for dinner. He nods and I stand, stretching to wake up more. I yawn before looking to Jer and moving to wrap my arms around his waist, resting my head on his chest. He wraps his arms around me to hug me back and I sigh as I wish I could stay here. But I know I can't and eventually I pull away from him.

"I'll see you later." I mumble and turn to leave but he grabs my wrist, pulls me back to face him and kisses me chastely on the lips.

"I'll see you tomorrow, love." He replies after breaking the quick kiss. I smile at that and nod before I leave the house. I walk across the lawn to my car, looking it over for any damage but it's perfectly fine, other than the scratch on the driver's door.

I still cringe at that scratch but don't fuss about it as I slide in. I start my beautiful, amazing car, listening to her purr before I pull out, contemplating briefly if I'm too obsessed with my car.

Nah, I just love this thing so much.

I park in front of my house tiredly and go up the driveway, across the path to front door. I walk in, getting assaulted by the smell of turkey and berries that make my stomach growl to remind me of the fact that I haven't eaten in a little over five hours.

"Levy?" Mom calls and I sigh, moving through the cool house to the kitchen that's slightly warmer than the rest of the house because the stove is on.

"Yeah?" I ask as I lean against the wall next to the silver fridge while Mom opens the oven to check the bird.

"Could you set the table? Also, where have you been? I can understand being gone yesterday but you've been gone most of today. What were you doing?" she curiously demands while squirting the baking bird with more baste out of the tray the turkey is cooking in. I'll admit, the entire turkey looks so gross with seasoning on top and juices running down its browning skin, but Mom knows how to make it taste amazing.

I pull my gaze from the cooking turkey to the cupboard where all the plates and bowls are positioned right above the silverware drawer. I move to grab three plates and the appropriate silverware before I go into the dinning room to set the table. I place the napkins under the forks and spoons and assure that each plate has a glass for water in front. I go back into the kitchen and slouch against the wall again.

"I was out with friends. I'm sorry I was gone so long, I'll try not to stay out that late again if you don't want me to." I finally reply to her question, though I don't specify which friends because I know she's assuming I was with Lydia and Jess, and she does not need to know the truth yet.

"It's fine, Levy, you have fun with your friends. Just don't do anything bad, okay. Stay out of trouble. Oh, would you get the wine from the fridge too? It's the white zin." She adds and I nod, not asking what the heck white zin is and instead look in the fridge for some kind of wine that I assume is clear.

Though, when I look I don't see any clear wines in the fridge. But I do only see one wine bottle and assume despite the pink hew that it's what she was referring to so I take the half empty bottle out of the fridge and put it on the table in the dinning room. I move back to the kitchen to watch Mom as she heats up some corn and green beans.

"Oh, I got an A for the shadowing project." I state, remembering that she wanted to know my grade when I knew. She stops stirring the corn to turn to me with a wide, proud grin.

"That's great, honey, I'm so proud of you." She coos and moves across the kitchen to pull me into a tight hug. I smile despite the fact that her small arms are somehow restricting my breathing and instead hug her small frame back.

"Thanks, Mom." I mumble. She pulls back to pat me on the shoulder before making an 'oh!' of surprise when the water in the pan of corn starts to boil over. She goes back to the stove to stir the corn, seeming to be focused on that so I just slink out to the living room where Dad is watching the baseball game on TV. It's a recording from the weekend, he always records the games in case we can't catch them on the weekend. I get the feeling he waited until today to watch it because I wasn't here on Sunday.

"Hey, kiddo, want to watch the game? The Dodgers are winning." He adds, motioning to the TV. I shrug and take a seat next to him to watch the game.

It's quiet other than the sounds coming through the large TV while we watch intently. After the last player misses the ball, and we cheer, Mom comes in to tell us dinner is ready. Dad turns off the TV and drops an arm around my shoulder.

"I haven't seen you in a while, it's nice to watch the game with you again. We missed the last few." He adds and I nod, knowing he isn't looking for an apology or anything so I don't say anything. We all sit down at the table, after Mom and Dad bow their heads to pray. I don't bother though, I honestly think that if there is some higher being, he probably knows I'm too hungry to wait any longer to eat so I can thank them for my food.

Though when Mom notices that I'm eating without following their foolish ritual she sends me a disapproving look. I ignore it though and enjoy the moist white meat of the turkey, barely tasting a hint of wine in the meat that I assume Mom marinated it with.

"This is good, Mom." I mumble past a bite of turkey before swallowing to take a large bite of potatoes followed by the candied cranberries.

"Thank you, honey, but don't talk with your mouth full." She chastises and I shrug, taking a sip of my water while Mom and Dad nurse a glass of wine each. "Did you tell your dad the grade you got for your project?"

I shake my head at that, making sure to take a large gulp of water to assure I don't have any more food in my mouth. Then I turn to look at Dad at the head of the table.

"I got an A." I state and he grins, putting his glass of wine down.

"That's great! I'm proud of you. See? You wouldn't have gotten such a good grade if you had been shadowing me, I'm too boring." Dad adds with a chuckle. I shake my head in disagreement but really I'm thankful I didn't shadow my dad.

It was inevitable that I meet Jer at one point, as I doubt my mom would ever leave that job and one day I would go to the office to talk to her or something and no doubt meet him. However, if it weren't for this assignment, I would never have spent so much time with Jer and gotten to know him better.

I never would have met Ian because I wouldn't have been at the cafe that day working on my paper. And I wouldn't be with either of them, I wouldn't be as happy as I am now if I did shadow my dad. I put my fork down at that thought, taking a break from devouring my plate of food as I imagine my life without either of them.

I can't imagine it though, despite the truth that I have only known them a little over a month. I haven't known them more than a blink in the whole scheme of things yet I love them both so much; the thought of not knowing them makes my heart clench in pain.

I brush those thoughts away and pick up my fork to continue eating so neither of my parents ask me if everything is okay.

"Would you like a sip of the wine to celebrate?" Dad asks and Mom smacks him lightly on the shoulder.

"Don't offer our minor alcohol." She scolds and he shrugs, extending his glass to me. I take it with a shrug, already used to this. Not that they give me alcohol all the time but when I do something well-or when it's a holiday-they tend to offer me drinks of wine or champagne to celebrate. I don't understand the logic but I don't bother questioning it.

I take a sip of the clear pink wine, handing the glass back to my dad as I swish the bitter-sweet liquid in my mouth to 'fully appreciate it' as Dad says. It's not bad, better than the weird yellow wine my aunt gave us that, according to my parents, was pretty cheap stuff. It's not as good as the rich Merlot red wine my parents received from a coworker a year or two ago though.

I swallow the wine and eat the remainder of my turkey, opening my mouth to say something about the wine but the doorbell rings followed by knocking. I look between my parents in confusion to see if they invited someone over but they look just as confused as I am.

"Hm, I wonder who that is." Mom muses, getting up and wiping her hands on her blue jeans. She leaves the dinning room to answer the door but isn't gone more than a minute before I hear her heals clicking against the hardwood floors of the hallway. She comes back into the dinning room but doesn't sit down. "Levy, there's a dark haired boy with really light gray eyes at the door, he asked for you. He seems kind of...off. Do you know him?" she questions as she clasps her hands on the back of her chair.

"Oh, yeah..." I trail, standing from my seat quickly, not providing any explanation. I move through the hall to the front door and open it to reveal a swaying Ian. His brown hair is a tousled mess and his usually bright gray eyes are glazed over and bloodshot. My brows furrow in confusion while he seems to take a minute to comprehend it's me at the door.

He opens his mouth to say something, probably in greeting, but instead hunches over and releases the contents of his stomach in my mom's pink azalea's.

Chapter Twenty-Seven

{ Chapter Twenty-Seven}

"Ian," I gape, moving to wrap my arms around him before he can collapse when he finishes vomiting, covering my mom's beautiful pink flowers in brown foamy chunks. The sight of the chunks makes me gag as it reminds me way too much of the turkey I just consumed, and the mashed yams. I shudder and pull Ian's shaking body into the house so I don't offend the poor flowers any more than they already have been.

"Ew," he manages to mumble as I close the front door, looking around to make sure my parents didn't come check on me. I let Ian lean against my door as he groans quietly and wipes his mouth with the back of his hand, wiping his hand on his dirty gray uniform slacks.

"Ian, what are you doing here? Wait, what's wrong?" I ask, looking him over once more. No wonder Mom said he seems off. There's definitely something wrong with him, it's obvious by the way he's swaying, the vomiting, the bloodshot eyes. If I didn't know better I'd assume he's drunk, but how would he get drunk? His dads don't seem like the type to have alcohol lying around. And if they did, surely they would have it locked away, or keep it somewhere safe. Why would he get drunk though?

"'M fi-ine." He mumbles, his words slurred and my eyes widen.

"Ian," I hiss, looking around the room again in paranoia that my parents will come in. "Are you drunk?" I demand.

His glossy gray eyes meet mine and they begin to water, making my own widen in surprise.

"Sorry, Le-Lev-eee." He slurs softly and I shake my head.

"Don't apologize to me, you're the one who's going to have to explain to my mom why her azaleas have chunks on them." I muse with a laugh to lighten his mood so he won't start crying, I don't want to see him cry because of me.

"Can I stay--" he groans, closing his eyes before continuing with them closed. "Here?"

I don't ask why, I know if he went home in this state his dads would freak out on him. I also know that's the last thing he needs considering he's obviously emotional so I nod, reaching out to take his wrist but he yanks it away quickly, ramming his elbow into the door in the process.

"Sorry," he mutters while I stare at him in surprise.

"It's okay, babe." I murmur quietly and he opens his eyes to look at me with sadness in his pretty gray eyes. He extends his hand, though it's shaky and he obviously is seeing double because it's not really aimed at me, more to the side of me. I take it though and lock our fingers, leading him away from the door.

He stumbles but I keep him up and lead him through the house, thankful that the dinning room isn't open to the hallway or else Mom and Dad would see Ian's drunken state and question me about it. Not to mention that they would question me about Ian in general, of course they'll question me anyway but I'll worry about that after I get Ian safely up the stairs.

"Be careful on the steps." I warn and send him up in front of me, keeping one hand on the railing while the other stays on his back in case he falls back. We make it safely up the stairs though and I lead him to my room where he collapses on my bed.

"Is your stomach feeling okay?" I ask as I bring my small waste basket from beside my dresser to the side of my bed in case he throws up again.

"Mhm," he hums and I nod, pulling my sheet over his body.

"Okay, I'll be back in a minute with a glass of water and a cool rag. I want you to stay here, don't leave my room. The bathroom is right through that door if you need it and it's only connected to my room so no one else will come in. I also have a trash can right here in case you feel sick again so if you have to puke do it in there. I'll be right back." I assure before giving him one more glance as I leave.

I make my way back down the stairs and into the dinning room where Mom is just collecting the plates and silverware; Dad being the one to collect the leftovers. I clear my throat while they clean up and they glance at me.

"Um, my friend is here, I was wondering if he could stay the night. He uh, just got in a fight with a friend and doesn't want to go back home." I lie, feeling horrible for doing so but I can't exactly tell my parents that one of my lovers is drunk in my bed for an unknown reason.

"Oh, of course he can stay, honey. But doesn't he have school in the morning? I know you do, and if you plan to stay up all night and skip school you better think twice. I will drag you out of bed tomorrow if you don't get up." She adds sternly but I wave her off.

"I won't stay up all night," I assure though I'm almost positive I'll be getting up a lot tonight to tend to Ian.

"Well, if it's okay with his parents than he can stay. I don't need a worried mother ranting to me that her son didn't come home tonight." She mutters with an eye roll. I chuckle at that, until I actually imagine Owen calling my mother. I shudder but push those thoughts out of my mind.

"You definitely won't get a call from a worried mother." I reply, pondering the idea of telling her she probably doesn't want to look at her flowers tomorrow, but she nods so I make a note to tell her tomorrow when she freaks out. I smile and after I get a cold glass of water for Ian, I head back to my room. Ian is still in the same position I left him; groaning with his face buried in my pillow.

I close my door, turning the lock in case my parents try to come in. I walk across to my bed and lay my hand on Ian's back hesitantly. When he doesn't flinch or get upset at the contact I begin rubbing soothing circles on his back.

"Ian, babe, drink some water. Try to finish the glass, it'll help." I murmur, placing the water on my nightstand. He turns over to look up at me before his eyes slowly move to the slightly tinted glass holding water with a small pink bendy straw in it.

He mumbles something inaudible to my ears, that I honestly doubt were actual words before he reaches out with a shaky hand to grab the glass. He brings it to his face as he attempts to sit up a bit though he's barely sitting up at all. He moves his lips to try to take the straw between them but after many failed attempts, I guide the pink plastic to his plump pink lips. He takes it and gulps from the straw quickly, not seeming to give any pause as he drinks all of the water in the glass. When it's empty he shakily puts it on the nightstand before his eyes falls shut while he falls onto his back again.

I run my fingers through his stringy hair, dampened by sweat. He seems to smile slightly at that until I sigh and he opens his eyes.

"Why did you get drunk?" I ask, pulling my hand away from his hair. He stares at me for a while, either to think of a lie or to try to remember the truth. I hope it's the latter, I don't want him to lie to me about this.

"Him." He mutters, his eyes falling shut again but I get the feeling he's closing his eyes so I can't read them. I don't ask for any explanation because I know he's talking about his ex, which makes my heart clench followed by protective anger pulsing through me at the thought of his ex contacting him.

"Did you talk to him?" I ask, trying to keep the anger out of my voice because I'm not angry at Ian, I'm angry at the piece of shit ex of his and I don't want Ian to think I'm mad at him.

"No," he replies before I can think of all the ways I would kill the man if I ever met him. Relief washes through me though, pushing some of the anger away. I start to ask what happened but he interrupts me. "Had a dream 'bout him. I was there again. He was there." He mumbles, his voice shaking.

"Where did you get the alcohol?" I ask, changing the subject slightly so he doesn't start reliving that night as I get the feeling the alcohol will make that more likely.

"A friend's brother." Ian replies and I nod though he can't see me as his eyes are still closed. I watch the steady rise and fall of his chest, the occasional twitch of one of his fingers. Then I sigh.

"Babe, look at me." I order softly, resting my hand against his cheek. He opens his glossed over, bloodshot, gray eyes to stare into my own boring hazel ones. "You can't get drunk again, or take any illegal drugs either. I can't begin to imagine how you felt when you did, and I understand you were upset, but don't ever do it again. Please. This isn't good for you and I don't want to worry about you drinking. So please, please, don't do this again." I whisper, biting my lip.

"It helps," he mumbles and I bite my lip harder, tracing my thumb over his cheek down his strong jaw, feeling the obvious stubble he failed to shave today.

"It doesn't help, it makes everything worse. Please, promise me you won't get drunk again. At least not until you're old enough." I add pleadingly and his lips twitch in a smile.

"I'm old enough to drink in other countries."

"Ian," I groan. "Promise me." He stares at me for a while before nodding slowly.

"'Kay, promise." He whispers and I smile, leaning down to kiss his cheek, feeling the same stubble against my lips.

"Thank you." I say when I pull back, heaving a sigh of relief. Then I glance down at his clothes, recalling that he wiped his hand, which had vomit on it, on his already dirty gray slacks. And his white dress shirt--a shirt I've seen him wear as part of his uniform--is filthy also, the white stained with what I assume is dirt with alcohol from the smell of it. It makes me wonder where his jacket and tie are, but I don't ask.

"Hey, I think you should change. I doubt you're comfortable in that. I have some pajama pants and an old band shirt you can borrow to sleep in." I add, getting up to retrieve the items from my dresser.

"Sorry I puked on the pink flowers." Ian says and I laugh as I turn back once I have the plaid pajama pants and Metallica shirt in hand.

"It's okay, babe. Now come on, I'll help you to the bathroom so you can change." I add, moving back to the bed where I drop the clothes on his lap. I help him sit up but he shakes his head, leaning in to drop his head on my mid-chest.

"I can't." He mumbles, sounding apologetic.

"Do you want me to help?" I ask as soothingly as I can to make him feel better. He nods against my chest so I nod to myself while he pulls his head off my chest, looking up at me.

"Alright," I nod once more and bite my lip. I reach down to unbutton his shirt, sliding it off and trying not to stare at his strong chest, a hint of hair sprinkled all over his chest with a trail leading into his slacks. I clear my throat and pick up the shirt, helping him slip his arms through the appropriate holes before pulling the faded black fabric over his head.

I swallow and move to unbutton his pants but he shakes his head, doing that himself. I simply help him stand, letting him clutch my arm in a death grip as he slides his uniform pants off, leaving him in simple black briefs that I quickly avert my eyes from. I reach down to grab the red plaid pajama pants, also faded, and help him slide them on. They're a bit big on him but they stay on so that's all that matters.

"Do you have to wash these some special way? Or are they machine wash-able?" I ask dumbly, referring to his dress shirt and gray slacks. He lies back in my bed, snuggling up with my extra pillow before yawning.

"Machine." He mumbles in the pillow and I nod, taking the clothes in my arms along with the empty glass. I put the clothes in the washer first, adding the soap and setting a timer on my phone so I'll know when to switch the clothes to the dryer, then Ian will have clean clothes tomorrow. Then I go back into the kitchen to refill the glass with more water.

I place the full glass on the nightstand once I'm back in my room and have the door closed. I smile at Ian and lean down to kiss him on the forehead lightly before I go into my dresser for some pajamas of my own. I pull out black sweats and a Guns 'n Roses shirt my dad gave me a few years ago before I go into the bathroom to take a shower.

I turn the water to warm, enjoying the warmth it provides to my body. I finish with the shower pretty quick so I can be with Ian in case something happens. I change into the pajama pants and over sized shirt before I leave the bathroom.

When I reach my room, putting my dirty clothes in my hamper, I realize Ian is sleeping. His breathing is even, his arms clutching my extra pillow tightly to his chest with the sheet barely drawn over half his legs. I smile a bit and put my keys, phone, and wallet on my nightstand next to Ian's phone. I realize before I turn out my light that it would probably be a good idea to call Ian's dads, one of them anyway. Haiden.

I pick up Ian's phone because I don't have his dads' numbers, and hope he doesn't have a lock on his phone. Thankfully he doesn't so I go to his ICE contacts, assuming his dads will be listed and they are. I call him and hope he doesn't get mad at me for Ian staying here. The line rings three times before it's picked up.

"Ian, where the hell are you? Do you realize how late it is? Do you know how worried your father is right now? You leave the house this morning and haven't come home at all, God only knows what could have happened to you." Owen answers and I close my eyes, shaking my head as I pray to God that Owen won't come kill me.

"Um, actually, Ian is asleep. He came over to my house about half an hour ago. He was uh, upset. I don't really want to wake him up." I mumble, looking at Ian's relaxed sleeping form.

"Levy, of fucking course. What do you mean he's asleep? Why is he at your house? Why haven't you brought him home?" Owen demands icily and I cringe.

"He just fell asleep. He wanted to see me, I guess. But he's kind of feeling under the weather. I think it's food poisoning." I add but then widen my eyes when I realize I probably should not have told Owen that Ian is sick.

"He's sick?! He needs to come home. Where do you live? I'll get him right now." Owen growls.

"No, no. He's okay, I think it was just mild food poisoning. He threw up in my mom's flower bed. I honestly think it's best if he stays over tonight. I'll take him home early tomorrow or take him to school if he wants. He'll be okay here." I assure. There's a pregnant pause that makes me wonder if Owen will even agree, followed by muffled voices that I assume belong to Owen and Haiden.

"Fine, fine, fine. He can stay the night. But I swear on my father's grave, if he comes back with a single scratch, or comes back upset, I'm going to kill you." Owen snaps in irritation but I know he's just worried about Ian.

"Thank you, thank you so much." I sigh in relief until he speaks again.

"But I want to talk to him. To make sure he's okay." Owen adds. I stare at the far wall before hanging my head because I should have known it wouldn't be that easy.

"Okay," I reply because I can't exactly fight with him. I put the phone down on the dresser and tap Ian but he doesn't make any move to show me he's awake.

"Babe," I whisper, sitting down on the bed next to him and shaking him slightly. He lets out a long groan but his tired, glossy eyes open to look at me expectantly.

"Whaa?" he huffs.

"Owen wants to talk to you," I state, lowering my voice. "Try not to sound drunk." I add and he nods, seeming a bit more alert.

I hand him the phone and he yawns, blinking twice.

"Daddy?" he answers and I bite my lip at that, smiling. He clears his throat and nods slowly. "I'm good, just tired. What? I wanted to see him."

There's a pause and I can hear the distant, distorted voices through the phone. Ian yawns again and nods, shutting his eyes.

"I know. I love you too. I'll be home after school tomorrow." He manages without slurring or pausing, or stuttering, and he hangs up. He puts the phone back on the nightstand before his eyes fall shut and his breathing starts to even out.

"Ian," I try, realizing he's still holding my pillow to his chest, while using my other as, well, a pillow. Of course he's asleep before I can get him to give me the pillow so I just drop my head in defeat. I get up and move across the room to my light switch. I shut the light off, blinking but not moving as I adjust to the dark.

When I can make out most of everything I slide into bed, but realize with a heavy sigh that I have to go change Ian's clothes to the dryer or else they won't be dry for tomorrow. I enjoy the comfort of my bed for a little longer before I get back up, moving through the dark room and ramming my foot into what I can only guess is the end of my bed.

I swallow any curses I may have uttered to the bed and instead limp to my door. I open it, go back to the laundry room where I wait another five minutes for the washer to stop before I toss the clothes in the dryer, checking the tags to make sure neither the shirt nor pants have to be air dried or something.

I make it back to my bed after that with no more run ins with inanimate objects and slide into the bed next to Ian. I lay my head on the mattress, closing my eyes but I know I won't be able to sleep without a pillow. So, with yet another sigh, I open my eyes to the bleak darkness.

"Ian." I call, shaking him lightly but he's already snoring lightly, and I really don't want to wake him up when he's actually sleeping. So instead I manage to pry my pillow from his tight grasp, laying it up by my head. I sigh and wrap my arms hesitantly around Ian's relaxed frame. When he doesn't do anything in response I relax and close my eyes.

"Goodnight babe, I love you." I whisper quietly.

When I'm nearly asleep in that not-quite dreaming state, I distantly feel his hands clutch mine. Then I finally fall into the peaceful sleep.

Chapter Twenty-Eight

{ Chapter Twenty-Eight}

The next morning I wake up to someone calling my name quietly. I huff and push my nose deeper into the intoxicating scent that I now easily recognize as Ian.

"Levy, get up." I feel someone tapping my shoulder so I finally open my eyes. I realize my face is buried in the crook of Ian's neck while his arms are tightly coiled around my left arm which is draped over his waist. I carefully pull my arm out of his grip to turn over so I can see just who is bugging me. It takes me a minute to realize it's my mom who's standing at the side of my bed with an arced brow.

"Yeah?" I ask with a yawn.

"You need to wake up, you have to be at school in an hour." She chides quietly and my brows furrow in distaste.

"Right, yeah. Okay." I mutter, sliding out of bed. I leave my room with her hot on my trail as I go to the laundry room.

"Who is sleeping in your bed?" Mom demands once we're in the laundry room. I shrug as I open the dryer to get Ian's now dry slacks and shirt.

"My boyfriend." I mutter dryly. I close the dryer and move to the kitchen to retrieve some breakfast for Ian. Of course Mom follows me while I look in the fridge, deciding to just get him some cereal. I pour the fruity cereal into a bowl and add milk before putting the milk back. I also go into the cupboard for the noproxen I know we have in case Mom or Dad go out with our aunt.

I find the small bottle and take two of the blue pills from the bottle, putting them in my pocket before placing the bottle back in the pantry.

"You have a boyfriend?" Mom asks in surprise and I finally turn to her. I pick up the bowl of cereal along with the clothes in my other hand and nod.

"Yes,"

"And he stayed the night..." She trails, an uncomfortable look crossing her face that makes me blush and look away.

"Oh God, no. He was just upset and feeling under the weather so he slept over." I assure, my face blazing at her assumption.

"Oh, good. Well, I have to go to work, honey. But I'll see you later. Your father already left, don't think about skipping school though. If you do you can't have friends over for a week." She adds sternly and I nod. I put the bowl back down on the table and move across the kitchen to give my mom a tight hug.

"I'll see you later, Ma." I say and pull back. She nods with a toothy smile before exiting the kitchen. I take the bowl in my hand again and carefully move back up to my room. Ian is, surprisingly, sitting up in bed awake.

"Hey, babe." I greet as I walk in, placing the bowl on the nightstand. He groans, rubbing his temples.

"Shh," he hushes and I silently laugh before taking the noproxen out of my pocket to hand to him.

"Take these, they'll help your head." I say in a whisper and he nods. He takes a large swig of the water before putting the pills in his mouth and swallowing.

"Thank you." He says, his voice raspy. I nod and motion to the bowl on the table.

"I didn't know what you would want but cereal is easy so I just got you some of that. I hope you don't mind it's a sugar cereal." I add. He shakes his head and begins eating it gratefully while I place his clean clothes on the bed in front of him. I move to my dresser to pull out a pair of tight black jeans, a less faded Metallica shirt, and a pair of clean black boxers.

"I'm sorry about your mom's flowers." I hear Ian say from behind me and I turn to him with a grin, completely forgetting about that. I probably should have told her when I gave her a hug but considering I didn't hear a traumatized scream I assume she hasn't noticed.

"It's okay, I don't mind. They weren't that pretty in the first place." I assure with a shrug. He nods slowly as he takes another bite of the cereal. I drop my eyes though and bite my lip. "Just don't do that again. Well, don't get drunk, you can puke in my mom's flowers again if you want." I add and receive a small twitch of a smile from Ian.

"I won't. I'm sorry I worried you." He replies and I nod, moving across the room to kiss him on the forehead.

"Finish your breakfast, I'll give you some mouthwash after I get dressed." I state and go into the bathroom. I change into my clothes then pour some mouthwash into a small cup after I brush my teeth and go back to my room. Ian finishes the last bit of milk from his bowl before taking the mouthwash and gargling, moving to the bathroom with his clothes where he spits it out and gets dressed.

"Levy," Ian calls while I grab my things off my nightstand, checking my phone for any new messages. I turn to him, only now realizing that he moved from across the room to right in front of me.

"Yeah?" He hugs me tightly, resting his head on my shoulder with his nose against my neck.

"I love you." He mumbles against my skin and I smile, hugging him to me just as tightly.

"I love you, too." I reply. We stay like that for a moment but soon I pull away and kiss him on the cheek. "Come on." I urge, handing him his slim phone that he shoves into his pocket before I take his hand.

We move through the house and after I lock the door behind me we get in my car. Ian directs me to his school which isn't too far away. I park in front of the school behind a silver van and Ian thanks me but I reach out to grab his wrist before he can leave. He turns to me in question and I smile.

"I'm going to pick you up after school, I want to talk to you and Jer." I add before I lean over to kiss him. I move my lips with his, savoring the sparks that ignite my body as our lips meld together. He pulls away, slightly out of breath, and smiles with a light pink blush tinting his cheeks.

"Okay, I'll see you then. I can't wait. I mean, I can, but I don't want to. I will though. Um, yeah... I'll see you after school." He mumbles before he leaves the car and I notice a few people are staring at him as he takes the front steps two at a time. I get ready to get out and teach them not to stare in case they bug Ian, but they all seem to leave him be so I drive away.

I barely park in the school parking lot before the bell rings and I sigh as I realize I have to go all the way to the office to get a late slip now.

~ ~ ~

School ends up being boring. The teachers have started to remind us of prom and graduation but that's it. While Jess was out sick today and Lydia simply talked with me about random stuff, though the conversation also went to our relationships.

Nothing other than that happened though, and I'm thankful when the final bell rings. I sigh in relief and make my way out of the horrible building that I'll probably miss once I graduate. I drive first to Ian's school, parking in front and waiting for him.

After a couple minutes I see him midst the crowd of students wearing identical uniforms as him. Although he seems to be rebelling with his black Converse while the other students are wearing dress shoes. I watch as he scans the curb, his eyes lighting when they land on my idling car. He hops off each step, loosening the navy blue tie around his neck as he moves to my car.

He slides in, tossing his bag in the back and I greet him with a kiss on the cheek. I put the car in drive and pull out of the school.

"So where are we going?" Ian asks once he unbuttons the top two buttons on his dress shirt.

"Jer's office." I reply, already knowing my mom is gone. I park under the same oak tree when I get to the building, the leaves on the familiar tree sprouting for spring and offering some shade from the heat.

"What are we going to talk about?" Ian asks though I wave his question off.

I had thought about it quite a bit during class, the fact that my mom now knows I'm with Ian. Then it occurred to me that no one knows about Jer, and though I don't think telling the whole town is a great idea, I think it would be best to tell our parents. They deserve to know, and they won't be as harsh as some people would.

We get out and I lead Ian into the office after checking for the receptionist's car-Julie! That's her name. I shake my head at that, realizing I couldn't remember her name for a better part of a month. Her white car is gone so we enter the building, cool air immediately envelopes us and chases away the warmth from outside.

Ian looks around in awe at everything while I lead him through the familiar building. I pass Mom's empty office and knock gently on Jer's door when we reach it. Jer opens with a smile when he notices us and ushers us in.

"Hey, I wasn't expecting you." He states, giving us each a hug. I shrug, moving to sit on the couch with Ian. I link my fingers with Ian's and motion for Jer to sit down so he takes a seat on the couch next to me.

"I want to tell our parents about us." I state, biting my lip. Ian stares at me and Jer drops his eyes but nods slowly.

"I think they deserve to know." Jer replies, though he sounds reluctant. I can understand that, I'm really scared to tell them, but like he said: they deserve to know.

"I think we should do it tomorrow." I add and both of them gape at me, their gray and gold eyes staring at me in disbelief.

"Wait, you can't tell your parents about this," Ian waves between the three of us before continuing. "On your birthday."

"I want to." I reply. Jer seems to be thinking of a way to convince me not to, but eventually he just nods.

"If that's what you want to do, that's what we'll do. I'm with you all the way, love." Jer assures and Ian squeezes my hand.

"Same here. I'm with you all the way...but I think you knew that. Yeah, that was pointless... I'll shut up." Ian adds and I chuckle.

"Thank you guys." I mumble and they nod. It's silent before Jer stands, looking down at us with a smile.

"Why don't you guys come over and we can watch a movie," he offers and I nod quickly as Ian does. So after Jer gathers his stuff and locks his office up we go to his house. Ian rides with Jer, apparently he likes Jer's SUV better than my baby, as if that's possible. When we get into the house Ian looks around in curiosity at Jer's house.

"Do you want something to drink or eat?" Jer asks as he slips his jacket off. I shake my head and take a seat on the couch while Ian looks around a bit before sitting down next to me.

"No thanks," Ian replies and Jer nods as he enters the living room. He turns the TV on and I grin when I realize he put on Ian's favorite movie-The Lion King. Ian grins and Jer takes a seat next to Ian, playing the movie.

It's calm and relaxing, so nice. To be with both of them, to just relax with them. It's so nice. And it only gets better when the movie is finished and I realize Ian is asleep on Jer. His head is resting comfortably against Jer's upper arm while his arms are wrapped around Jer's arm. I grin at that, resisting the urge to coo while Jer strokes Ian's hair comfortingly.

"I can't believe he fell asleep on you," I whisper, getting up from the couch to take a picture that I set as my background. Jer smiles down at Ian's relaxed, lightly snoring form.

"Me too," he replies, his smile turning soft before he looks back at me. "Should we wake him? It is getting a bit late." He adds. I sigh but nod solemnly. I know if I don't bring Ian home soon, Owen is going to murder me, he's probably freaking out already.

"Maybe we can get him in my car without him waking up." I reply hopefully but I doubt we can. We can try though. I wrap my arms around him and attempt to lift him but he mumbles incoherently before his eyes open to look at me tiredly.

"Sorry, babe, I have to get you home." I murmur. He yawns but nods, standing for himself but when Jer stands he opts to cling to Jer's arm. It's adorable. I lead the way to my car and Ian slides in after hugging Jer tightly, kissing him on the cheek.

"This was nice," Jer states, pulling me into his arms. I nod, moving to kiss him lightly.

"It really was," I agree and pull away. He locks his fingers with mine though for a moment.

"Happy early birthday, I may not remember to say it tomorrow. I'll talk to you later, love." He says and lifts my hand up to kiss my palm gently.

"I'll talk to you later, I love you, Jer." I reply before dropping his hand and getting into the car. I link my fingers with Ian's once I'm in the car and sigh as I drive. I won't be able to sleep tonight, I'll just be thinking of tomorrow. I'm nervous already.

Chapter Twenty-Nine

{ Chapter Twenty-Nine}

As I suspected I barely got sleep last night. After dropping Ian off and having a scary talk with his scary father telling me scary things, I went home. But I couldn't sleep. I fell asleep, had a bad dream, woke up, went back to sleep, woke up. It continued like that the entire night. I think I got a most of maybe four or five hours of sleep if I round up.

And school, despite my boredom of it, goes by way too quickly than I would like, I'd really rather prolong the day. Lydia of course gives me a present and a cupcake, singing happy birthday to me. She gave me a DVD, and a music gift card from Jess who's still out sick.

It all went by far too fast though and here I am, with Ian in my car while Jer walks out of his house. I contemplated telling Jer not to come as it might be better, especially when telling my parents. But the whole point of this is so we can be together freely so Jer has to be here, as long as he's okay with it which he's assured me numerous times throughout the day when I messaged him that he wants to be there. He gets in the back after locking his car and squeezes my shoulder in reassurance.

"It'll be okay, love." He murmurs and I sigh, feeling Ian's hand cover mine on the gearshift in comfort.

"I hope so," I mutter, pulling away from Jer's house and driving towards Ian's. We decided it's best to start with his because I get the feeling they already know what's going on, or at the very least suspect. Plus I know Owen is going to want to meet Jer. Though, it's also kind of a way to put off telling my parents. I'm so nervous I left the house for school an hour before I had to so I wouldn't bump into either of them.

I park in front of Ian's large house, his plush green lawn coming back quite nice for Spring. I turn off my car, run a hand through my hair and bite my lip.

"Come on," Ian urges, leaving the car. I sigh, glancing in the rear view mirror at Jer who smiles at me in reassurance but I see the nerves in his golden eyes. I don't comment though, instead I get out of the car with Jer behind. I lock her up and catch up to Ian who is almost at his door already.

Jeez, for a kid who's almost always nervous, he doesn't seem nervous to tell his dads that he's in a relationship with two guys. He walks right into the house without hesitation and I honestly envy his confidence at the moment.

I link my fingers with Jer's and lead him into Ian's house. I close the door behind us while Ian leads the way to the living room where his dads are sitting in silence. Haiden is reading a book while Owen is reading some papers with a blue pen hanging from his lips. He pulls the pen from his mouth and circles something on the paper before Ian clears his throat. Haiden looks up in surprise but Owen doesn't look away from the papers.

"I was wondering when this day would come." Owen states and I laugh despite myself. His unamused bright green eyes bore into me but I don't reply. His eyes move back to the papers and makes a mark with the pen on them again.

"Dad, this is Jer. He's uh, with us." Ian pauses, a blush moving from his neck to the tips of his ears. "I mean, not with us as in our friend, he's um..." He trails, clearing his throat. "In a relationship with us. A romantic relationship. Like, polyamorous. That's the right term, right?" he whispers the question at me and I nod so he nods.

"Polyamorous. Yep, that's what it is. I hope you're okay with it because I'm happy and I don't want you guys to be mad. I mean, they make me really happy. And uh..." He shifts from foot to foot as he tries to continue to ramble but I think for once his nerves aren't allowing him to ramble. Not much anyway. Owen puts his papers on the table while Haiden closes his book.

"Do they really make you happy? Do they promise to take care of you?" Owen demands, looking between Jer and I. We both nod in assurance but he continues to stare between us. "You realize my son is seventeen for the next four months?" Jer nods.

"Yes sir, but I have not and do not intend to have sexual contact with your son while he's still underage." Jer replies calmly but his hand clutches mine tighter. Owen stares at Jer for a few minutes before rolling his eyes.

"Sure you won't. Look, I love my son more than anything else in the world, even more than my husband--"

"Hey," Haiden interrupts him but Owen simply leans in to kiss Haiden briefly before continuing as if nothing happened.

"I love him to death, I would gladly die for him over and over. And if he gets hurt, I get pissed. Which is why I would never do anything to take away his happiness, I'll always try to keep him happy within reason." He says in closing. Haiden rolls his eyes, looking between the three of us.

"He's giving you his blessing in his roundabout way. But do be advised that if either of you hurt my son, I will do worse then simply shoot you with my twelve gauge shotgun as my husband would do. But as long as you keep my son happy, I'm happy." Haiden explains with a smile. Owen grumbles about how Haiden is always ruining his fun but they don't say much more. They have us stay for a bit so they can interrogate Jer but eventually we manage to stand to leave.

To my house we go.

I shudder at the thought as Ian hugs both his dads. It makes me smile to see big bad Owen melting into a big teddy bear when he hugs Ian, his lips pulled into a soft smile while he ruffles Ian's hair. Then we leave. I drive five miles under the speed limit to prolong the talk with my parents. Sure, Ian's were okay with it, but they're different. They're more accepting than mine, and I know because of Ian's past that they care even more to make him happy.

Much to my horror I somehow get to my house faster than I thought I would. I nearly groan at that but instead turn the car off and get out with Ian and Jer. I move over to the lawn, lacing my shaking fingers with Jer's and I realize he's shaking as well, but he looks much calmer than I'm sure I do. I reach out for Ian's hand and clasp his in mine, he's not shaking but I can tell he's nervous. And I know why. This is the real thing.

And I'm so nervous, my stomach is tying itself in knots, making me nauseous. Nevertheless we walk up to my front door and I drop both their hands, knowing it would be best not to walk in there flaunting our relationship. Holding hands would be just as bad as coming in with rainbow signs and chanting some weird but catchy chant.

I walk into the house with them behind me and hope my parents are in the living room. They should be because they spend a couple hours each day in the living room after work before they clean the house or make dinner.

Thankfully both of them are in the room. Dad is watching a show called Cops, something I grew up with and though I didn't like it for a while, I grew a fondness to it. Mom is half watching the TV, half reading something on her phone.

"Uhm, Mom, Dad." I call and they look over to me. Mom's eyes fill in confusion when they land on Jer.

"Jeremiah, what are you doing here? Levy, what's wrong?" Mom demands in utter confusion. I feel my body tremble more and I feel my eyes sting but I ignore it, wondering how Ian was so calm when telling his parents.

"Mom, Dad. I have to tell you guys something and I don't want you to get mad. Please." I add. They nod but it doesn't give me a lot of reassurance.

"Of course, what's wrong? Honey, why is Jeremiah with you?" she adds, sounding so utterly confused.

"He's with me. Us. I mean, we," I motion to Ian, Jer, and myself. "We're together." I add.

She still looks confused though.

"Together? What do you mean?" she asks. My eyes move to my father's, and he looks slightly less confused. Then her eyes widen but I clarify nonetheless.

"We're in a relat--"

"No," she snaps, standing quickly and her eyes snap from mine to Jer's, determined anger potent in her eyes. She makes a move towards Jer but Dad quickly grabs her wrist to keep her from moving.

"Sheryl, you can't attack him." I barely hear Dad whisper into her ear. She growls and clenches her hands into fists as she glares at us.

"Levy, honey, I understand if Jeremiah pressured you into this. I understand. Just tell me he did." She adds, practically pleads. I shake my head though, taking a step back so I'm between Ian and Jer. Ian immediately takes my hand to link our fingers and Jer hesitantly does the same.

"He didn't pressure me into this. I wanted this. I love them." I reply honestly and despite hoping for the best, I can see the decision in her eyes.

"Get out of my house right now." She orders. I stare at her in horror. Of all the worst outcomes I thought of, this wasn't one of them, this never crossed my mind.

"Mom," I choke just as my dad calls her name. She rips free of my dad's grip and moves across the room faster than he can react. I take a step foreword, moving protectively in front of both Ian and Jer in case she tries something. But she stops in front of me with a firm glare in place.

"You're not welcome here anymore. When you decide to quit this sick relationship, if that's what you want to call it, then you can come home. But as long as you continue to live like this, you aren't welcome in my home. And you," she turns her glare to Jer. "You make me sick. Expect my resignation letter on your desk tomorrow morning. I hope you realize before it's too late that this isn't right. Now all of you, get out of my house." She growls. I see my dad over her shoulder, looking so conflicted, but I don't expect him to stand up to my mom. I know he loves me, and that's all I care about.

I nod numbly but I don't budge. Instead I bite my lip and stare into my mother's angry, disgust filled hazel eyes, the same ones that she gave to me, the same ones she looked at me with infinite love with not twenty-four hours ago.

"I love you," I say before I leave the house with Ian and Jer right behind me. I get in my car and after both of them follow suit I pull away. I drive but I don't know where I'm going. Eventually after a good ten minutes of silent driving, mostly around the block, I stop at a stop sign. I stare ahead before it hits me.

I choke on a sob, putting a hand against my mouth to cover the next but it doesn't help. I can't do anything to stop the tears or sobs, or the snot. I shake and cry, realizing that my mother hates me. I don't have anywhere to go, everything is still at my house save for a few things. I don't know what I'm going to do. I can't sleep in my car, I don't have money for a hotel because I know my mother is going to cancel my card as soon as she can. Oh God, I can't do this.

"Levy," I jump in surprise when I realize Jer got out of the car and has my door open. "Love, get out. You can't drive like this. Come on." I nod shakily, trying to put the car in park but I can't seem to so Ian does it for me.

I get out and get into the back with Jer while Ian moves across the seat to drive. I cling to Jer and cry into his chest while he rubs soothing circles over my back.

"It's going to be okay, love, I promise." He whispers, kissing the top of my head and running his fingers through my hair. I can't bring myself to reply, I don't think I could if I wanted to, I can barely take breaths between the sobs.

I can't believe this happened. Was she right? Am I sick? Did I bring this onto myself?

The questions don't help, it just makes everything worse. I cling to Jer like my life preserver as my breathing comes in sharp gasps. My heartbeat accelerates as I remember my mother's words, the hate in her eyes.

What am I going to do? I don't have a job. I'm still in high school. I don't have money for anything. Pretty soon I'll run out of gas and won't even have my car. Oh God. I can't believe this is happening. This can't be happening.

"Love, calm down. Take deep breaths. Come on, breathe with me." Jer murmurs, breathing in deeply as an example. I do as he says though that only calms my breathing, I still can't stop crying. "It's going to be okay, love." He whispers, kissing the top of my head before my car stops.

"Come on, babe." I hear Ian soothe while Jer manages to get us out of the back without me having to let go of him. I feel Jer's arms around me and we stop for a minute, making me open my blurred eyes to see Ian pulling Jer's keys from his pocket. Then we continue to walk.

I hear a door open and close behind us followed by another opening of a door. Then I'm being sat down on something squishy, a bed, Jer's bed.

"Levy, come on, look at me." Jer orders softly and I open my eyes to see Jer and Ian in front of me. "Give me your phone and wallet then lie down."

I do as he says and shakily hand him my phone followed by my wallet. He lays the items on the bedside table and helps me lie down. Ian moves in behind me to hug me from behind while Jer slides in next to me so I can continue crying into his chest if I so choose. His black shirt is wet with tears, snot, and probably saliva, but I don't care. I clutch at him tightly and sob into his chest while both of them whisper reassurances.

Though I know they aren't sure of what they're telling me. They can't know that my mother will forgive me. They don't know any of that, they can't. But that doesn't matter because just being with them makes me feel better. It helps me calm down enough to murmur a quiet 'I love you' to each of them before I fall asleep.

Chapter Thirty

{ Chapter Thirty}

Two weeks has gone by.

Two weeks of talking briefly with Dad only to have Mom start yelling, making him hang up.

Two weeks of trying to keep my grades up so I won't compromise my graduation.

Two weeks of staying in Jer's bed, only getting out when I absolutely had to.

The first three days I was asleep. I took off school, wouldn't eat and only got out of bed to shower and use the bathroom.

The next three days I spent at school, using one day while Mom was looking for a new job to get some stuff out of my room. Mostly clothes because I know Dad would never let her throw anything of mine away.

The next three days after that I went to school, doing my homework and handing it in like a robot. Then it started. It was tiny comments I would brush off, just small things I would hear in the halls. Then it got worse. Within two days the school seemed to have somehow learned of my relationship, and everyone started to make comments that weren't even cleverly whispered.

They would comment things about being disgusting and sick right to my face. Even some of the teachers began to stare at me differently. So when Jer asks me this question while I'm eating some kind of soup Ian's dad Owen made and sent him over with, I can't help but nearly spit the soup on him.

"You want me to what?" I ask for clarification and he tilts his head.

"I want you to take me to your prom." Jer repeats.

"My prom. In the school? Where a majority of the school thinks I'm a pervert?" I demand in disbelief and he nods as if it's nothing.

"Everyone should go to their prom. And besides, you need to get out of the house-and not just for school. You need a distraction." He adds. I stare into his golden eyes, trying to think of an excuse not to go but I can tell he's worried and wants to get me out of the house. So I reluctantly nod and he smiles.

"Okay, I'll go I suppose." I mutter. He kisses me lightly before moving to change the movie.

"Good, you can pick up the tickets tomorrow and I'll get us something to wear." He replies. I nod in agreement, not bothering to listen to anything else he's mumbling as I close my eyes and enjoy my soup.

I only open them once more when the bowl is empty and Jer takes it from me. He returns from the kitchen and pulls me into his strong chest. I try to contain it but I sniffle, tears falling down my face faster then I can try to stop them. So I give up and cry into his chest until I fall asleep as I tend to be doing lately.

~ ~ ~

"Do we have to go?" I ask from the bedroom while Jer changes in the bathroom. I don't know why he's changing in there, I've seen him change before, but I don't question it.

"It'll be perfectly fine, love." He assures and I roll my eyes. He's said that exact line every time I asked the last two days. He seems pretty keen on going.

"Ian isn't going," I state with an overly dramatic sigh. Ian decided to get sick yesterday and tell me he can't make it but he hopes going will take my mind off things. He did it on purpose, he just didn't want to go. Lucky kid gets to eat Owen's amazing soup, stay at home, and probably read or do something fun.

I wouldn't be so opposed to going though if half the school didn't stare at me funny. I think it might be fun, but with everything that's happened, I'm not sure how fun it's going to be. But I'll do this to humor Jer, show him that I am okay despite the fact that I keep crying on him nearly every day.

"Jer, it's almost time to go and you still haven't given me my tux." I call, looking down at my bare body. He had me strip to my boxers before disappearing into the bathroom where he has yet to come out.

"Oh right. Your outfit is on the dresser." He calls back and I arc a brow at that but again I don't question it. I pull on the white button up followed by the tight black jacket and tight black slacks. A skinny tie is all that's left so I tie it quickly, turning as Jer walks out of the bathroom and I freeze.

"Oh my..." I trail, unable to even finish the thought as I stare at Jer. His lips turn in a smirk as he buttons the cuffs on his black dress shirt. A stylish black leather trench coat falls down his body to just below his knees.

Wearing tight black leather pants and large boots with straps and studs. He looks so amazing, I honestly just want to continue staring at him.

However he moves towards me and has me put on a pair of black dress shoes before taking my hand to leave the house. I still can't speak though, he looks so hot. So magnificent. He definitely makes up for having to deal with all the irritating people at school. I couldn't honestly care less about the school, not now that I've seen Jer.

"You, you." I try, but I still can't finish my sentence while we leave the house.

"I'm glad to know I've made you speechless, my love." He replies with a chuckle as he uses my keys to unlock my car. He gets in the driver's seat, making my brow twitch, but even so I can't speak. Finally, when we're halfway there I manage to choke something out.

"You look so sexy," I blurt and he laughs as he turns to the street my school is on.

"Thank you, love. As are you. Black suits you." He adds, reaching over to take my hand and brush his lips against the top lightly. He parks in the already packed parking lot and we both get out. I take Jer's hand once we reach the front of the car and then lead him the short way to the gym.

"Are you sure you don't just wanna go back home? 'Cause I gladly will. We don't have to do this." I add and he gives my hand a reassuring squeeze.

"I want to do this for you, love." He whispers. I don't reply but when we stop at the door where a bored looking female student is taking tickets, I freak out.

"Oh no, I think I forgot the tickets. And where are my car keys?" I hiss, patting my pockets.

"I have the tickets, and your keys." Jer replies with a small laugh as he hands the tickets to the girl who's staring at Jer in awe. She quickly takes the tickets though and lets us in so we go through the door.

And I'll admit, it's beautiful in here.

Stars are hanging from the ceiling, a disco ball and red, pink, along with black streamers are hanging up. A banner with 'Senior Prom 2016' is hung from the basketball hoop and a DJ is set up in the corner, currently playing some song I vaguely remember as some popular pop song.

"Wow," I breathe, looking around in awe. I had no idea this horrible room could be so pretty, but so it is. "It's beautiful."

We move across the gym to the refreshments but I feel eyes on me. Hundreds of pairs of eyes boring into the back of my head. I try to ignore it though as I take a sip of the sickly sweet blue punch and try so hard not to turn to look at the students but I fail. I turn briefly and see eyes filled with disgust and irritation, though a very select few just look bored.

"Jer," I mutter to him while he tries the red punch, pinching his face in distaste.

"Don't drink this one, they did something to it." He mumbles, dumping the rest of his red punch in the trash. He turns to face the students as I am but doesn't seem fazed. Rather he takes my hand when a slow song starts. I blink as he leads me through the crowd to the dance floor, pulling me into his body.

"Wait, what are you--"

"Come on, love, dance with me. I love this song, it's really quite romantic." He adds, putting his hands on my waist and pulling me closer. I look away from the eyes of strangers to look into Jer's, and I calm down, smiling.

"Okay," I whisper, wrapping my arms around his neck. We dance slowly to Kiss From a Rose by Seal, and while most of the other students do the same they continue to stare.

By the middle of the song I rest my head on Jer's shoulder, closing my eyes so I don't see their eyes. Though when the song is nearly ended, Jer pulls back to kiss me. I move my lips with his and savor this moment, ignoring everyone else as I enjoy Jer, as I enjoy this.

"Levy," he whispers once he pulls away, not paying any mind to the now fast paced song that everyone is jumping around to.

"Yeah?" I ask curiously.

"I love you so much," he replies and I smile so big, I didn't know it was possible to smile this much. "Now, what do you say we give these kids something to stare at." He adds.

"What?" I ask in confusion until I hear the beginnings of Closer playing by NIN. My eyes widen as a grin spreads across his face. "How in the world did you get this to be played?" I ask in surprise, looking around for the chaperons but they don't seem to be around.

"There may or may not be a small decoy by a bright pink haired girl in the hallway. And I may or may not have bribed the DJ." Jer replies, moving closer to me. I laugh and shake my head until he begins to grind against me.

"What are you doing?" I gasp, looking around at the students who look confused because of the song.

"Giving these kids a something to watch." He replies calmly, moving his hands from my waist to my ass that he squeezes. I blush but after he juts his hips out against mine, I relax a bit with a laugh. I turn around and grind my ass against his crotch while he holds my hips, kissing my neck and biting at it lightly.

All the while all my classmates gape at us and though I know I'm totally going to get more trouble because of this, I don't care. This is far too fun to pass by, and for once in two weeks I'm really smiling.

Things may not always be easy for Jer, Ian, and I, but if we can do this; if we can show the people who disapprove of our relationship that we don't care, we can do this. We can handle whatever these people throw at us. As long as we have each other.

That's all I could ever ask for. I don't need a big house or a lot of money, hell, I don't need to be close to my mother. As long as I have Ian and Jer, I'll be happy because they make me happy.

They're the men I want to spend the rest of my life with because I love them.

This is all I need.

This is all I want.

Epilogue

---

4 -4-16 {Epilogue}

"Levy, are you home?" I hear Ian call out and grin. I put my book down and take the stairs two at a time towards the front door.

"Babe," I coo, capturing Ian in a tight hug followed by numerous kisses placed all over his face, neck and arms. He laughs and pushes me off playfully but leans in to kiss me chastely.

"Where is Jer?" he asks, looking around the hall.

"He's still at work, he'll be back in about an hour. But how was it? Are you tired? Did they treat you well? Did you have fun?" I ask, taking one of his hands in mine while I use the other to grab his bag before leading him upstairs.

"It was great, I'm exhausted. They treated me very well, and I had a lot of fun." He replies with a laugh followed by a tired yawn. I don't blame him, he just got back from a two week book tour and signing for his recently published book.

I remember a no more than three years ago when he was writing up the first draft, he would have weird bursts of energy followed by times when he didn't want to do anything but focus on school. Then if he didn't get inspiration through the moments when he didn't want to get out of bed, he had mini fits of rage that I had no idea what to do with the first time it happened.

I remember there was one time he got so fed up with the lack of inspiration that he lit his recent chapter on fire, burning it in our bathroom. When I asked him why he would do that, and if he had it backed up, he told me he did not have it backed up and he didn't know why he was even bothering writing something that no one will ever read. Although I didn't--and still don't--fully understand what he's talking about, about making a difference, I get what he means. He wants to leave something behind that people will remember.

Of course in those times I couldn't do much but offer him a change of scenery and comfort him. Jer helped a bit more, taking him to places I would never set foot in--such as this old abandoned mental hospital a few towns away. But then he finished the first draft, and the second, and third until he sent a polished manuscript to a publisher. He was ecstatic that his book was published, it was nice to see him less emotional and more to himself.

Then he went on the tour and of course neither Jer nor I could go because we both have work. I missed him so much, and I know Jer will be happy to see Ian a day earlier than expected.

"Come on, lie down and take a nap. We can all talk about it later. If you want anything tell me," I add, leading Ian to the bed where he lies down. He clutches Jer's pillow to his chest and sighs, his eyes falling shut.

"Thanks, boo." He replies and I smile, leaning down to kiss him on the forehead.

"No problem, babe. Now get some sleep." I mumble, leaving the room after I turn out the light. I go into the kitchen and begin making dinner, knowing Jer will be back soon.

Halfway through making some mashed potatoes to go with our Tri-Tip, my phone rings. I wipe my hands on my black jeans before I take my phone from my back pocket. I glance at the caller ID real quick and a grin spreads on my face.

"Hey, Dad." I greet, jumping up to sit on the white marble of our bar.

"Hey, kiddo. How have you been doing?" he asks curiously and I shrug, keeping an eye on the boiling green beans to make sure they don't over-cook.

"I'm great, Ian just got home." I add with a goofy smile, watching the water in the black pot bubble slowly.

"Oh, he got home early? That's great. Do you and Jer have anything special planned for him?" I shake my head.

We actually were planning to invite everyone over for dinner when Ian got back, but everyone would be busy and I knew Ian would be too tired. So we decided to just make a nice dinner and bring out an expensive wine Victoria gave us one of the time she was over a few months ago with Lydia, her new wife.

"Nah, we decided to have a small dinner. We're going to open the Bordeaux Victoria gave us a few months ago." I explain, hopping down from the bar to stir the greens.

"Make sure to let it breathe. Did you catch the game?" I smile as I stir the green beans.

"Yes, oh my God, I can't believe we almost lost. Thank God for that save, am I right?" I add, shaking my head.

"Definitely. Oh I got Ian something for his birthday, I know it's a bit late but I'll drop it off tomorrow." He adds. I laugh a bit, realizing that he's a bit more than late with Ian's gift as his birthday was a bit more than a month ago, but I doubt Ian will care, we all know my dad has a bad memory when it comes to dates.

"That's great, I should be here, if not Ian will be for sure." I clear my throat and bite my lip. "How is Mom?"

There's a pregnant pause, allowing me to hear the distant sound of the newscaster on the TV Dad must have playing. Then finally I hear him clear his own throat and I can imagine him shifting uncomfortably as he does anytime I ask him about Mom.

"She's good, kiddo. She's been babysitting a lot for the neighbors, you remember them, right? The Petersons? Well, they recently adopted a new daughter and your mother has been over there almost every day for weeks to babysit." He explains with a laugh but we both know he's not exactly amused. We both know how sad he is that my mother refuses to talk to me, to even acknowledge my existence other than to remind me how disappointed she is in me for choosing this.

"That's great, I hope that kid turns out better than I did in her eyes." I mutter bitterly but immediately regret it.

"Levy," Dad starts and I sigh, dropping the spoon to the counter with a clank.

"I know, I know. She doesn't mean it, she'll come around, she loves me. It's been fifteen years, Dad, I don't think she's going to come around." I snap with another sigh, opening my mouth to continue about how my mother obviously does not give a damn about me if she doesn't even want to acknowledge my existence. But then I feel a pair of strong arms around my waist and I lean into them, relaxing slightly as Ian's smooth scent fills my nose.

"I'm sorry, I know you don't want to hear that." I say.

"No, it's not your fault, kiddo. But she does love you, you know." He replies.

"I know, of course she does." I assure, even if I don't believe it. I want my dad to be happy, I don't want him to be upset because of my mother. "Hey, Dad, I have to go actually. I have to finish dinner and Ian just woke up, Jer will be home in a few. I'll talk to you later though, I love you."

"I love you too, kiddo. I'll talk to you later. And I'll talk to your mom too." He adds. I smile wanly at that but nod.

"Alright, talk to you later, bye." I reply, hanging up and sniffing as I lean into Ian.

"Don't think about it," Ian whispers, brushing his slightly chapped lips over the sensitive skin of my neck. I hum with a small smile, reaching behind me to rest my hands on his hips.

"I miss her." I state.

"I know," he mumbles against my neck. He pulls away and turns me to face him, his lips turned in a smile. "What are you making?"

"Tri-Tip, mashed potatoes, and green beans. Oh, and we're opening the wine Victoria gave us a few months ago." I add, leaning in to kiss him as I push thoughts of my mother away.

"That sounds great, hon." He replies when I pull back to turn off the stove and pull the pot of green beans off the burner.

"The potatoes are a bit runny, but the meat is already great. Jer let it marinate over night and we used that one beer you like in the marinade." I explain, opening the oven to make sure the meat is cooling but not completely cooled.

"Yum, that sounds great. I can't wait to try it. I've been living off fast food." He adds with a shudder and I chuckle.

"Well, I can guarantee it will be way better than any fast food." I assure as the front door closes. I exchange a glance with Ian who grins. I laugh when he darts out of the kitchen to greet Jer and cease my stirring to listen.

All I hear is a loud 'ooph!' followed by a thud and laughter before Jer speaks.

"Babe, I didn't know you would be back today. God, I missed you." I hear footsteps move through the house into the kitchen and I turn to see Ian clamped around Jer's arm. I smile, putting my fork down and wiping my hands on my jeans. I walk across the kitchen to where Jer is still standing with his arm around Ian's waist and I smile, kissing Jer in greeting before hugging the two.

"Hey," I greet as he lifts my hand up to kiss the top.

"Hey, love. Is dinner almost ready? I'm starving, I had to skip lunch for a meeting." Jer adds, dropping my hand so I can go stir the potatoes a bit more.

"Dinner is ready, could you set the table?" I ask, not really aiming the question at either of them, just whoever wants to. They both do it together though, taking the plates and silverware before disappearing to the dinning room. I pour the green beans into a bowl, draining the water and putting the bowl next to the bowl of steaming mashed potatoes. I pull the Tri-Tip from the oven and move it to a clean tray, putting a knife on the tray.

I take the tray and move to the dinning room, placing it in the middle of the table where Jer and Ian are already sitting. I go back to the kitchen to grab the potatoes and green beans, placing them on the table also before I go back for the wine.

I take a seat at the dark red wood table and we begin loading our plates. For a couple minutes we're silent, the clinks of silverware on the black plates as we load the food on the plates. Though Ian pauses after he fills his plate and bows his head to pray but Jer and I start eating right away. Ian starts eating after he's done praying and we start talking about Ian's book tour, Jer's recent deal with a large high end clothing store, and a few of the recent cases I've had at the law-firm.

It's casual and nice as we pour the wine after it breathes. After dinner Jer helps me with the dishes while Ian migrates to the living room, turning on the TV to play some soft music while he reads. I wipe my hands off when I place the last plate in the dish drainer. I follow Jer into the living room where Ian is lounging on the couch with a book in hand. I move to take a seat but Jer's fingers lock with mine, pulling me into his body.

I arc a brow up at him in question and he smiles. He slips his other hand around my waist, moving down to grip my ass.

"Dance with me," he commands and I chuckle, dropping my head as I shake my head.

"Why?"

"This is nice music." Jer replies, swinging us around in a circle. I laugh and move my hand around his neck and he grins.

"Okay," I reply with another round of laughter as he spins us again. He moves me away, pulling me back into his chest in a cheesy slow dance type move. By now Ian has perched on the couch, his book forgotten, to watch us in amusement.

After a few more spins, a girly twirl, and a run in with the wall, Jer finally stops in the middle of the room. I assume he's content with the stopping, until he dips me and I yelp in surprise, barely able to hold my footing as Jer looks down at me. He pulls me back up and plants his lips on mine lovingly, his arms dropping to my waist as he kisses me with so much love, so much passion.

And I smile, distantly remembering myself wishing I had exactly this fifteen years ago. I wanted to just dance with my partner, have fun. I have that now, with Ian and Jer, I have exactly what I wanted fifteen years ago and I can't begin to thank God enough, because everything worked out.

I know we'll always have problems, people will still look at us in disgust when we walk through town. But as long as I have them, I don't care about anyone else; everyone in the world can hate me, my mother can hate me, as long as I have Ian and Jer I can handle anything. We can handle anything.

{The End}

www.ingramcontent.com/pod-product-compliance
Lightning Source LLC
Chambersburg PA
CBHW072014210726
48294CB00011B/720